# PIPPA AND THE
PONIES

'Pippa! Come quickly! Hero's missing!'

Hero, a spirited black gelding, had only
been on loan to Pete for a couple of days
when he vanished. And this had happened
on the very night he and Pippa had
mounted guard on their ponies to try and
catch red-handed the mysterious nocturnal
riders.

They join forces with a group of friends in
the search for Hero, and the Easter holidays
are suddenly filled with excitement,
mystery – and suspense!

*The fifth book in the Pippa Pony series*

# Pippa and the Midnight Ponies

Judith M. Berrisford

**KNIGHT BOOKS**
Hodder and Stoughton

*For Sara. May she grow up with as keen a sense of humour as her grandfather, Edmund.*

Copyright © 1985 Judith M. Berrisford

*First published by Knight Books 1985*

**British Library C.I.P.**
Berrisford, Judith M.
  Pippa & the Midnight Ponies.
  — (a Pippa Pony Book: 5)
  I. Title
  823'.914[J]    PZ7

ISBN 0 340 36654 0

---

Printed and bound in Great Britain for Hodder and Stoughton Paperbacks, a division of Hodder and Stoughton Ltd., Mill Road, Dunton Green, Sevenoaks, Kent (Editorial Office: 47 Bedford Square, London WC1B 3DP) by Hunt Barnard Ltd., Aylesbury, Bucks.

# Contents

| | | |
|---|---|---|
| 1 | Pete's horsy surprise | 7 |
| 2 | 'Hello, trekkers!' | 11 |
| 3 | The hidden cove | 17 |
| 4 | Caught by the tide | 22 |
| 5 | Riders in the night | 28 |
| 6 | Friends or foes? | 33 |
| 7 | 'Phone the police!' | 39 |
| 8 | We need help | 44 |
| 9 | The mystery deepens | 50 |
| 10 | A message from Mark | 56 |
| 11 | 'Is that really you?' | 62 |
| 12 | Conspirators | 67 |
| 13 | What should we do? | 74 |
| 14 | A pony to hide | 80 |
| 15 | Not fit to ride | 86 |
| 16 | An unexpected clue | 92 |
| 17 | Trotting through the dark | 99 |
| 18 | Happiness for Mark | 104 |

# 1

## Pete's horsy surprise

'Good pony, Magic! Now let's try it again.'

Keeping my body as still as possible, I nudged my chestnut mare into a canter. Magic struck off with her near-fore and I moved my right leg back a fraction, pressing it against her side to prevent her hocks swinging out as she turned.

My pony obediently bent herself into the first tight circle of a figure-of-eight. Unfalteringly she carried out the change of leg in mid-air and again reminded me how lucky I was to have such a super pony.

Magic wasn't always perfect, of course. What pony is? She had her wilful moments. However, she had been partly trained in dressage when she came to me and now, after more than eighteen months' hard work and schooling, she was becoming all that any pony-crazy girl could wish.

Riding-mad though I had been for years, I'd never had a hope of owning a pony until the fateful day when my twin brother, Pete, and I had rescued the famous dressage apaloosa, Blitzen, from the sea.*

We hadn't known, of course, that the pathetic, salt-caked animal was an internationally respected

*See *Pippa's Mystery Horse*.

horsy hero. We'd called him Comet because of the white splashes on his chocolate-coloured coat, and in spite of many difficulties we'd hoped to keep him for our own. In the end we'd learnt his true identity and had discovered his real owner. I'd been heart-broken at the thought of giving him up, but my grief had been turned to incredulous delight when Madelena von Hoven had given me Magic – an impeccably-bred Welsh-Arabian – as a surprise consolation.

I'd had Magic for nearly two years now and every day I'd grown to love her more. She seemed to know and trust me, too. For the first time I was beginning to realise the full rapture of being what the books described as 'at one with my pony'.

Musing happily on these lines, I was taken by surprise when Magic swung out of her careful circle. She threw up her head, gave an impatient buck and, snatching at her bit, cantered towards the hedge.

'Hey!' I protested. 'Naughty pony! What do you think you're doing?'

I shortened the reins and threw my weight into the saddle to stop her. Then an unaccustomed whinny from the lane made me as impatient as my pony to find out who the newcomer might be.

Trotting Magic more sedately towards the hedge I heard my brother, Pete, coo-ee.

I reined up at the gate and, to my astonishment, saw my twin astride a striking-looking black geld-ing of about 14.2 hands.

'Hi, Pippa!' Pete called excitedly. 'Look what I've got.'

'Super!' I gasped. 'Who does he belong to?'

'Me, for the time being.' Pete looked pleased. 'Meet Hero. He's on loan to me for the whole of the Easter holidays.'

'Terrific!' I approved. 'But whoever lent him to you?' I looked appraisingly at the handsome black. 'I thought I knew every pony in the district.'

'Hero's only just arrived,' my brother explained. 'He belongs to a fellow at my school – Mark Cooper. Mark's mother and father are separated. His mother's thinking of marrying again, but Mark doesn't get on with his stepfather-to-be. His real father has taken a job in the Gulf, and he bought Hero for Mark as a parting gift before he left. Now Mark's mother and his stepfather-to-be are off to spend three weeks on a Greek island, taking Mark with them.'

'So Mark had to find someone to look after Hero,' I nodded. 'Fancy having to be parted from such a magnificent pony, even for a holiday in Greece.'

'Mark didn't want to leave him.' Pete shortened his reins and patted the black's neck as the pony sidled impatiently. 'In fact, I had a job persuading him I could manage Hero. His mother wanted to send him to the local livery stables but his stepfather said it would cost too much. Then they offered to lend him to a riding school in return for his keep but the proprietor said he wasn't really quiet enough.'

My brother broke off as the black waltzed sideways.

Doubtfully I eyed the two of them. Pete had never been as pony-mad as I was and, although he was good at most sports and had plenty of nerve, I

9

couldn't help feeling he was lacking in experience of handling a difficult pony.

'Don't look so foreboding, Pippa.' Pete managed to bring Hero to a standstill. 'Hero's only a pony, after all. It isn't as though I'd made myself responsible for a thoroughbred stallion and, anyway . . .' he smiled disarmingly, 'with a pony-expert like you on hand, how can I go wrong?' He glanced at his watch as Hero began to toss his head with impatience. 'It's almost lunch-time. Let's go and show Hero to Mum. We'll ask her to put up a picnic. Then, this afternoon, we can join Dave and the farm visitors on an afternoon's trek. That should get rid of some of Hero's high spirits.'

'Fine.'

I turned Magic towards the gate. With Hero ahead, spooking at shadows, and Magic beginning to jig with excitement, I followed my brother towards the cottage, trying hard to stifle a premonition of pony-disaster.

# 2

'Hello, trekkers!'

'No more nonsense!' I scolded Magic as I slid her saddle into place and buckled the girths, getting ready for the afternoon's ride. 'If you'll only be sensible and not get hotted up at being with Pete's new pony we'll be able to have some lovely times.'

My pony bent her head as if to listen and I felt the brush of her velvety lips. She nuzzled the back of my neck as I tested the stirrup leathers. It was as though Magic was letting me know that she understood.

Next moment, Hero's hooves clattered on the paving as Pete led him out of the stable where he had passed the lunch-hour. At the sound Magic threw up her chestnut head. Her nostrils flared. She danced sideways impatiently and I almost lost my reins.

I sighed. 'Try and keep Hero calm, Pete,' I called as my brother led the skittish black gelding into the lane. 'He's unsettling Magic, prancing about like that. If we're not careful he'll undo all my training.'

'Oh, forget about dressage for once, Pippa,' Pete panted as he hopped after the circling Hero. 'Relax and enjoy the ride.' He turned his head. 'Here come Dave and the farm visitors. So just settle down to have a good time.'

Easier said than done. I managed to get on my pony's back but, before I had found my stirrup, Magic began cantering on the spot. Impatient to join the other ponies, her neck muscles became hard and she began frothing her bit.

'She's never been like this before over the farm ponies,' I groaned. 'It's Hero that's having the unsettling effect.'

'Magic'll get used to him,' Pete said cheerfully. 'Tell you what, I'll ride ahead. You keep Magic back and let Dave and the trekkers follow me. That way there'll be plenty of distance between Magic and Hero.'

Pete rode the black on to the cliff path. My pony fretted and danced as I held her back and I wondered whether we were being foolhardy in following the narrow track. Then the trekking ponies drew nearer and Magic seemed to become calmer. Dave's stolid Welsh cob, Cloud, and the two half-bred Exmoors, Russet and Pippin, were old friends. Their presence seemed to assure Magic that we were setting off on one of our usual placid rides.

'Hi, Pippa!' Dave nodded a greeting before turning his head towards two jean-clad girls astride the trekking ponies. 'Meet Sharron and Tracey.'

'Hello!' I said. 'Welcome to Somerset.'

The two fair-haired girls, who were obviously sisters, smiled rather shyly and the elder, Sharron, said: 'It's lovely here, isn't it – a bit different from Streatham.'

'You're lucky to live here all the time, and to have such a beautiful pony.' The younger girl watched Magic a little apprehensively as my pony tossed her head, impatient now to be off after Hero. 'But I don't think I could manage her.'

'She's not usually so difficult,' I explained. 'It's just that my brother's been loaned a new pony. Hero's rather excitable and it seems to have infected Magic.'

'I hope it won't make Pippin play up, too,' Tracey's hands tightened nervously on the brown pony's reins.

'No fear of that,' Dave assured her quickly. 'Both Pippin and Russet are "patent-safeties". My Dad wouldn't let me take you out on them otherwise.'

Dave led the way forward along the cliff path followed by Tracey and Pippin while I kept Magic a safe distance behind Russet.

Sharron glanced uneasily at the steep slope below the path.

'Done much riding?' I called to take her mind off the jagged rocks in the sea below. The track was quite safe and the two half-bred Exmoors were real 'schoolmaster' ponies and as sure-footed as mountain goats. However, I knew that to ride along the edge of the cliff might be unnerving to some people. 'Do you go to a riding school in Streatham?'

'Sometimes.' Sharron warily kept her gaze on the path ahead and I could see her relax a little as she answered my question. 'It costs too much to have proper lessons, but Tracey and I muck out and clean tack some Saturdays in exchange for rides, whenever things aren't too busy.'

'Mum said it was best to save the money and spend it on riding here while we were on holiday.' Tracey turned in her saddle to add her bit. 'It was so Sharron and I could go riding that she and Dad chose the Garlands' farm.'

'And a good thing, too,' I said warmly, knowing just how life in Streatham must be for the two sisters and how pony-deprived they were. It had been like that for me up to a couple of years ago, until Pete and I had gone on a pony-trekking visit to an aunt in Scotland where we'd become mixed up in the rescue of a stolen racehorse. Then we were given a course of riding lessons at our local stables as a reward.* What bliss life here was in contrast to that, with a super pony of my own like Magic and acres of wild moorland to ride!

We turned on to the moorland now and, as Pete reined Hero up ahead, Dave turned to the two girls. 'Like to try a canter?'

'Please.' Sharron gave a relieved smile as her mount left the cliff path.

'O.K., then.' Dave called to Pete to hold Hero back until the girls were well past. Then, leaning over to put a hand on Pippin's rein, he nudged Cloud into a rocking-horse gait. The younger girl settled comfortably to Pippin's rhythmic canter and, with a relieved slackening of his lips, Dave let go of the half-Exmoor's rein. Both girls seemed reasonably confident and Hero was moving restlessly and champing his bit, so, when Pippin and Russet were past, my brother let the black follow.

*See *Pony-Trekkers Go Home* and *Sabotage at Stableways*.

14

Hero snatched at the bit and, despite Pete's efforts to hold him in, broke into a headlong gallop.

'Hold hard, you ass!' Dave glanced over his shoulder at the sound of the thudding hooves but Pete was past and away.

The half-Exmoors wanted to follow but they were seasoned trekking ponies – beginners' mounts – and the sisters managed to hold them back. Not so Magic. Already impatient at being made to bring up the rear, my pony fought her bit.

'Steady, girl. Hold hard!' I shortened my reins.

Magic pulled after the others so I turned her in an attempt to circle. My pony dug in her toes, then gave an unseating buck and I lost a stirrup. While I was groping for it she broke into a gallop.

Before I could regain the iron, Magic had passed Dave and the girls and was well after Pete. So, settling down to enjoy myself, I drove my pony on.

'Right.' I touched her with my switch. 'If you're determined to gallop, you can.' We were approaching the steeply rising ground of Dunkerton Beacon and I forced her to keep up her pace. 'This should take the tickle out of your toes.'

Pete and Hero were well ahead but, to my surprise, we seemed to be gaining on them. Never before had Magic shown such a turn of speed. Her tail was streaming, her hooves fairly flying over the springy upland turf.

My pony was fast, really fast. This was wonderful. Hitherto I'd been so busy working at dressage that I'd never realised her potential. If she could jump as well as gallop she'd do well against the clock.

The ground became steeper. Ahead Hero was

15

slowing but Magic kept up her pace. Her neck was streaked with sweat. Her nostrils were showing red. Her flanks were heaving but she kept on, determined to overtake the black.

At last we drew level. I reined up Magic and she and Hero stood, blowing companionably, waiting for Dave and the two sisters to arrive.

'What a super ride!' Tracey gasped as they halted beside us. She gazed at Magic. 'My goodness, your pony can go!'

'Can't she!' Dave smiled hopefully. 'If Magic keeps up that standard and with Pete on Hero, we three could enter the team race at the Riding Club trials.' Then he looked rueful. 'That's if I could manage to borrow something faster and with a bit more "punch" to her jumping than Cloud.'

Sharron looked envious. 'It all sounds such fun. I wish we lived somewhere like this and had lots of ponies to ride.'

'Never mind, Shar.' The younger girl was more philosophical. 'We're here for a fortnight, so let's make the most of it.' Tracey turned eagerly to Dave. 'Where are we going to picnic?'

'I was keeping that for a surprise.' Dave's eyes twinkled at her enthusiasm. He looked from Pete to me. 'It's somewhere even the twins have never visited. Let's face it; few people know the place, even those who were born in these parts.' His voice took on a mysterious note. 'It's called the Hidden Cove. You'll see why when we get there.'

# 3

## The hidden cove

'It doesn't look much like a cove to me.' Pete shaded his eyes against the sun as we descended the zig-zag path to the beach. 'It's just an open stretch of sand.'

Dave chuckled. 'We're not there yet. This is just the approach.'

'Then the Hidden Cove must be somewhere beyond those rocks.' Tracey bounced in her saddle with such excitement that the stolid Pippin broke into a shambling trot.

'Look out, Tracey! Keep him back!' Her sister Sharron's voice rose and I saw her fingers clench on Russet's reins to pull him away from the edge.

The half-Exmoor was too staid to do more than shake her head in protest, but my pony caught the alarmed note in Sharron's voice. In sudden panic, Magic shied, put her off-fore foot on a loose pebble, slipped and nearly came down. However, she quickly recovered and soon we were on the beach heading for the line of jagged black rocks at the end.

Feeling the firm sand beneath her feet, Magic tossed her head. I looked enquiringly at Dave.

'A bit of a canter won't do any harm.' He cast an approving glance over his farm guests. 'Tracey and Sharron are well up to anything that Pippin and Russet are likely to do. So carry on. Take it easy, mind,' he warned my brother as Hero began to dance excitedly. 'No more flat-out gallops.'

This time it was Magic who let us down. Taking me by surprise, she snatched at her bit, bucked and set off at a wild canter.

I circled her determinedly. 'What's got into you?' I scolded. 'You were making such good progress and now you're a disgrace.'

I glanced back at Pete. With a tight rein, he was trying to check Hero who was cantering on the spot.

'It's all the black's fault. If you're going to carry on like this we shan't be able to come out with Pete and Hero. I'm not going to let fifteen months' training go to waste,' I reprimanded Magic as she sobered enough to allow the others to draw level. Then she set off again, galloping for the jagged rocks that spread across the beach.

I threw my weight into the saddle and tugged at her reins.

'You've got to stop sometime,' I told my pony exasperatedly. 'Those rocks are too high for you to jump. You'll have to pull up and wait for Dave to show us the way.'

Magic snatched obstinately at her bit. The rocks ahead loomed sheer and she seemed to be making straight for them.

At the last moment she swerved, making for a gap that had suddenly appeared. Desperately I clung to her mane, trying to keep my balance and at the same time tucking my knees out of the way of the granite rocks on either side.

'The Hidden Cove!' I gasped as we emerged on to a sunlit horseshoe of sand. 'And very well named. It's been very clever of Dave to bring us here. We couldn't have a more perfect place for a picnic, so just behave yourself, my girl, and don't do anything to spoil things for us all.'

Dave showed us a stream of fresh water where the ponies could drink. We ran up our stirrup leathers, knotted our reins and fed the ponies slices of scrubbed carrot. Slackening the girths, we left the ponies to doze in the sun while we settled in a semi-circle, backs against the rocks, to enjoy our picnic.

Afterwards Dave suggested we rode through the shallow water. 'The salt's good for their legs,' he told the girls.

However, Hero did not want to go into the sea. He tossed his head and circled, trying to pull away. Pete shortened his left rein and, using his legs, forced the black into the wavelets that were lapping the sand.

Still fighting the bit, Hero backed towards Magic who curtseyed away, drenching us both with spray before stumbling on to an unexpectedly soft patch of sand.

Irritated, I rounded on Pete.

'Keep that menace out of my way.' I jerked my head towards Hero.

'Oh, forget it!' grumbled Pete. He turned to Dave and the girls to say, maddeningly: 'Pippa's in one of her awkward moods.'

Ignoring his gibe, I touched Magic with my heels, trotting her through the shallows. 'I'm going ahead,' I called back over my shoulder to Dave and the girls. 'I don't want this dumb cluck . . .' I glared at my brother, 'to let Hero ruin all Magic's training.'

Dave called out something that I could not catch, so I trotted showily on, the droplets of spray from my pony's hooves making rainbows in the Easter sunshine.

Dave shouted again and I gave an airy wave. I supposed he was warning me not to go too fast in case the trekking ponies decided to follow. He need not worry, I thought. Pippin and Russet were as reliable as old jodhpur boots, and both Sharron and her younger sister had shown themselves more than capable of keeping the two trekking ponies in check. Besides, the far side of the cove looked interesting. There were the remains of a rough, stone jetty, tide-pools and sheltered places between the rocks that would trap the sunshine later on. With summer boating and bathing picnics in mind, I wanted to investigate.

'Come back, you idiot!'

Suddenly Pete was galloping along the beach after me, followed surprisingly by Dave and the girls.

'Turn back, Pippa!' Dave called.

'I won't be a minute,' I shouted as I drew level with the stone jetty. 'I want to take a look at this end of the cove. There's plenty of time before we need to go home.'

'Don't you understand, Pippa?' Dave yelled. 'You're riding into danger. Come out of the water right away.'

Most of his words were drowned by the splashing of Magic's hooves but I caught the note of alarm in his voice. Signalling to the others to keep back, I turned my pony's head shorewards. Too late!

All at once the ground seemed to go from beneath us. Magic plunged forward. Then, finding herself in two metres of water, she threw up her head.

I was wet to the waist but I did not panic. Most ponies swim instinctively and, although to my knowledge, Magic had never before been in deep water, there was no reason why she should be the exception.

'It's all right, pony. Keep calm.' Leaning forward to reassure her, I lifted her head with the reins.

Magic did not strike out as I had expected. Instead she bent her head. Her forelegs thrashed. The water churned but she made no progress.

'Something's wrong!' I called frantically to the others. 'Her hind legs seem to be trapped.'

To my horror, Magic's head was now even lower in the water. I slipped into the sea to support her. As I did so, I noticed something dark and sea-weedy looped in the green depths below.

'A rope's caught round Magic's fetlock,' I shouted. 'Come quickly. Magic's going to drown!'

# 4

## Caught by the tide

Magic's fore-feet thrashed. Desperately she plunged her head into the water as though trying to reach down to bite herself free from the restraining rope.

'Steady, Magic! Steady!' Dodging her threshing hooves, I tried to get near enough to raise her head above the waves.

The tide was coming in. Gradually the water was rising. Magic was trapped by a leg and I knew that, somehow, we must untangle the rope.

'Help!' I called to the group on the shore. 'Help! Magic's drowning!'

'Hold on, Pippa. I'm coming!' Letting Hero's reins trail, Pete ran along the jetty to jump into the water.

The tide was running strongly and he had to fight his way against the current. Dave was not far behind though Pete reached us first. Hanging on to Magic's saddle while he got his breath, he held out an encouraging hand to Dave.

'Help Pippa keep the pony's head up, Dave. I'm going down to see if I can free Magic's leg.'

Taking a deep breath, my brother upended himself to dive deep. Magic tried to flinch away from his kicking legs but the rope held her fast.

Pete seemed to be underwater a long time. Then

he surfaced, shaking the salt drops from his eyes and gasping for air before plunging again.

Dave and I could see him through the sunlit water. He was struggling to stay down as he tugged at the restraining rope.

'It's no use.' Pete spluttered as he surfaced again for air. 'Magic's fetlock's held tight. The rope's old and slimy and it's frayed a bit, but it's not rotten and I can't get it to part. We need a knife.'

'What's the hold-up?' Sharron waded into the water from the beach. 'Shall I ride for help?'

'There's no time.' Pete glanced at the water creeping its way up Magic's neck. It was all Dave and I could do now to keep her head clear of the water. 'We need something sharp. Try to find a jagged stone.'

Suddenly Tracey gave a whoop and began running over the slippery rocks by the jetty. The sun's rays glinted on a green glass bottle lying on the sand beside the old jetty.

'Careful!' Dave struck out for shore. 'Don't try to break the bottle, Tracey. Wait for me!'

Water poured from his clothes as he stood on the worn stones of the jetty to break the bottle. Carefully he wrapped a chunky piece of glass in his handkerchief and tucked it gingerly into the breast-pocket of his shirt before plunging again into the water and swimming back doggedly.

Again Pete dived. Air bubbles broke on the surface as he struggled to cut through the rope.

At last Magic kicked out, free. Pete rose to the surface sucking a cut finger. With Dave and me grasping each side of my pony's bridle near the bit and with Pete hanging on to a stirrup leather, we swam gently, letting the tide carry us ashore.

'Well done!' Sharron and Tracey were patting the soaking boys on their backs while I mopped uselessly at Magic with my sodden handkerchief. My pony was safe but exhausted. She began to shiver uncontrollably.

'It's a death-trap, there.' Shaken, I glared at the deceptively calm water beside the jetty. 'There ought to be warning notices. To look at it, you would never think there could be such a treacherous gully.'

'Dave tried to warn you!' Pete looked up from wringing out his jersey.

'Yes, Dave and I shouted like mad,' Sharron confirmed. 'Here, Pippa . . .' She held out her anorak to me. 'Take off your wet jumper and wear this. Otherwise you'll get pneumonia.'

The boys and I dried ourselves as best we could while the two sisters held the ponies. Our jeans clung clammily to our legs as we climbed back into our saddles for the long ride home.

'What I don't understand,' puzzled Pete, 'is how the gully came to be there.'

'It's the outlet of the stream,' explained Dave. 'Over the years it's been deepened. The smugglers used it in Victorian times. Then there was a rumour that a German U-Boat came in during the war to take off a spy. Since then the boatmen from Croom have kept the channel open. In calm weather they run trips to the beach for bathers and picnic outings.'

Pete nodded. 'Last summer I saw a board near Croom Harbour advertising the trips.'

'Well, there ought to be a Danger notice here,' I

declared firmly. 'I'm going to get Daddy to tell the coastguards about it. This place is a menace. I can't think why no one's bothered to put up a warning before.'

'Hardly anyone comes here by land; that's why,' Dave pointed out. 'Unless they've been on one of the boat trips no one would know there was a beach here. That's why it's called the Hidden Cove, remember.'

'I wish it had stayed hidden as far as I'm concerned,' I said. 'Magic'll be lucky if she doesn't get a chill.'

'So will we all.' Pete touched Hero to a trot. 'Best try to warm ourselves up a bit.' He turned to me with brotherly sternness. 'I don't know what's wrong with you, Pippa. Being your twin, I don't expect any thanks for saving Magic but you might be a bit more gracious to Dave. Without his help you wouldn't have a pony to worry about.'

'I'm sorry, Dave,' I said. My teeth chattered as the wind from the moorland penetrated my damp clothing. 'I owe you a very big "thank-you". You too, Pete.'

'I only hope this doesn't mean you won't come with us when Dave takes us out trekking again,' sighed Tracey. 'The ride and the picnic were such fun.'

'Until everything started going wrong.' Her elder sister looked sober. 'I hope Magic doesn't come to any harm from this afternoon, Pippa. Shall you get the vet to her?'

\*     \*     \*     \*

'Best not to panic,' Dave advised Pete and me before leaving us to ride through the farm gateway. 'With a good rub down and a bran mash, Magic may be as right as a field of clover by morning. See how she is, anyway, before you go calling out Mr Priestland.'

It was after seven o'clock when Pete and I reached the cottage and Mummy and Daddy were looking out for us.

'Indoors and into a hot bath with you, right away!' Mummy said firmly after feeling my still-wet jeans. 'Pete can have the shower.'

'What about Magic?' I tried to evade my mother's hold. 'She needs looking after. What about her?'

'I'll see to Magic,' Daddy said firmly. 'We'll put her in the stable for tonight. Hero's quite dry. He won't come to any harm in the field. I'll put on the kettle to make Magic a mash while you have your bath.'

'Be careful not to give it to her before it's had a chance to cool,' I warned.

'We won't,' Mummy assured me.

'And, Daddy . . .' I lingered in the doorway to call after my father as he led the ponies away. 'You will stay with Magic until she stops shivering, won't you? Keep wisping her down, and you may have to pull her ears.'

'Bath, Pippa!' Mummy pulled me into the cottage and shut the door. 'Your father and I have had to cope with plenty of pony emergencies over the last two years. You can give us credit for a little horse-sense. Now upstairs with you; and you're not to come out of that hot water for at least ten minutes.'

Steam was already drifting from the shower room as I passed. There was little need for Pete to be concerned about Hero, I thought enviously as I dropped my soaked jersey on to the linen basket and turned on the hot tap. Hero hadn't almost drowned. Pete could afford to leave it to Daddy to turn the black into the field. Pete could forget all about Hero until he was warm and dry and had eaten his supper. On the other hand I knew I wouldn't have an easy moment about Magic until the next morning proved her none the worse for her watery fright.

If we'd known how things were to turn out neither of us would have had a minute's peace that night!

# 5

## Riders in the night

To my relief Magic soon calmed.

Daddy said she had broken into a sweat twice after he had first rubbed her down. Then, each time he wisped her, he pulled her ears gently and talked calmingly to her until she relaxed.

My father insisted on staying with Magic until Pete and I had eaten our supper. Then he called me out to spend half-an-hour with her before I went to bed.

With a warm and comforting bran mash inside her and a hay net at which to pull, my pony seemed contented to doze. Not wanting to disturb her I didn't stay even for the full half-hour that Daddy had suggested.

Mummy packed Pete and me off to bed early but I couldn't sleep. I found myself trembling as I recalled the afternoon's events.

From Pete's room came the sound of pop music played softly on a transistor and I knew that he was as wakeful as I.

It must have been almost two o'clock before I slept and then only to relive the fright of Magic's near-drowning in my dreams.

My own shouts woke me from the nightmares, and it took me several minutes to realise that I was actually awake. Moonlight was streaming into my bedroom and the thin tapping of the honeysuckle against the window-pane made an eerie sound.

From across the fields Glen, the Garlands' sheepdog, barked. Hero whinnied from the field near the house. Could there be poachers around? Not wanting to go back to sleep right away in case I had another nightmare, I listened hard.

An astonishing sound met my ears. It was the clop of hooves in the lane.

Who could be riding at this time of night? I pulled back the curtains to look.

I was too late to see much – just a glimpse of a grey rump and the whisk of a silvery tail disappearing round the bend in the lane. Had Cloud and the trekking ponies – as disturbed as the rest of us by the day's happenings – somehow got out?

From the lane came the sound of flurried barking. I sighed sleepily, reassured that Glen was on the job. From past experience of straying animals I knew that the Garlands' well-trained farm sheepdog was more than able to cope.

Satisfied, I snuggled under my duvet. This time I dropped into a seemingly dreamless sleep.

\*　　\*　　\*　　\*

Next morning Mummy let me oversleep, so I woke in a panic to find my watch reading nine-twenty-five.

Magic! Dragging a comb through my hair and without bothering to wash or brush my teeth, I pulled on my jersey and jeans.

'Where do you think you're going?' Mummy's voice from the kitchen halted me on the bottom stair. 'You've no need to worry about Magic,

Pippa. Daddy went out to her at seven, before he made our early morning tea. He gave her a feed and turned her into the field.'

'But what about Hero?' I ran to the door. 'Yesterday it didn't seem as if he and Magic were going to get on. I don't want either of them to kick.'

'Don't fret, Pippa.' Pete's voice came cheerfully from the sitting-room where he was watching a Saturday sports-preview on the TV with a cup of coffee in his hand. 'Magic and Hero are getting on fine. I've been out to check. There's no need to flap so you can go back and wash your neck!'

I was just finishing my muesli when a couple of short barks from Glen heralded Dave's arrival at the cottage.

'I say, you two,' the usually imperturbable Dave sounded excited. 'What do you think's been happening?'

'Cloud and the trekking ponies got out.' I recalled how I'd been awakened from my nightmare the previous night.

'Half-right,' Dave acknowledged. 'The ponies didn't *break* out. They couldn't have. Dad and I've been round the fences and checked for gaps. There aren't any – and the gate was shut.'

'And where did you find Cloud and the ponies this morning?' asked Pete.

'In the lane. Glen's barking roused Dad. He looked out of the window, saw the ponies in the lane and got up to turn them into the field.'

'There must have been a gap somewhere,' argued Pete. 'Your Dad must have missed it in the dark.'

Dave shook his head. 'I double-checked with Dad this morning. Somebody let the ponies out.

That's what happened. What's more, the ponies had been galloping. There were streaks of sweat caked on their coats.'

'Hooligans!' I gasped, horrified, recalling the trouble our local riding stable had suffered during our town days at Dormhill.* 'Some louts must have let the ponies out and chased them. Still . . .' I thought back to the previous night, 'they weren't galloping when I heard them – just trotting. I even caught sight of Cloud's rump as she rounded the bend.'

'They'd been ridden,' said Dave. 'The yobbos even had the cheek to go into our harness room and borrow the bridles. We found them flung over the fence this morning. Dad says he's going to lock everything from now on.'

'Quite right,' I nodded, 'and I shall put Magic in the stable every night.' I stood up. 'I'll ride down to town this morning and get a padlock.'

'Magic!' snorted Pete. 'She's all you ever think about. What about Hero?' He looked thoughtful. 'Do you think there might be room in the stable for two?'

I shook my head. 'I'm not risking putting a half-trained rodeo animal like Hero in with Magic. Hero will be safe enough in the field. No hooligan could catch him, let alone get on his back to ride.'

Pete turned hopefully to Dave. 'Have you got room at the farm? I don't want to take any chances. Hero's only mine on loan and he cost Mark's Dad a packet. Apart from that Mark thinks a lot of him; and I wouldn't want anything to happen to his pony.'

'Sorry,' said Dave. 'If there was anywhere, Pete, you could use it, you know. As it is, Dad's put the

*See *Sabotage at Stableways*.

spare generator into our only loose-box and, with your Dad using the big stable as a workshop, there just isn't any place at all. Besides,' he added, comfortingly, 'this is probably a one-off thing. I've heard about vandals riding ponies at night near the cities but this is the Somerset coast. There aren't any built-up areas near here.'

'There's a boys' camp over the moor at Minton,' Pete pointed out. 'The boys there come from inner-city areas. They might get up to any sort of petty villainy.'

'They're well supervised though,' said Dave. 'Dad knows Mr Foster who's in charge and they were talking about it in our house the other night. Mum asked Mr Foster to supper and he was telling Dad what a good crowd of lads they'd got – no trouble at all, so far. Dad was even thinking of inviting some of them over in twos to trek. Then Sharron and Tracey arrived and they're so keen to ride that the ponies are fully booked for the week.'

'Perhaps some of the boys got wind of that and decided not to wait to be asked,' I suggested.

'Once they've helped themselves to the ponies at night, they'll do it again,' Pete predicted. He looked across at Dave. 'I don't want to take any risks with Hero. I think we ought to stay up tonight and watch.'

'Me too.' I was ready for any adventure. 'But Mummy and Daddy will never let us stay out at night.'

'No need to tell them.' He dropped his voice with a warning glance in the direction of the kitchen where Mummy could be heard stacking the breakfast crockery. 'We'll wait until they're asleep and then creep out.'

# 6

Friends or foes?

It was cold and creepy that night as Pete and I waited in the farm lane by the gate for Dave.

Clouds covered the moon and there was a chill in the wind that Pete said foretold rain. Under my duffle coat I was wearing my thickest sweater and I had on my cords. Even so I felt shivery and had to swing my arms to warm up.

'Ssh! Somebody's coming,' Pete warned as I stamped my feet.

There came a sudden beam of light in the farmyard as a torch was switched on and off. Then there were muffled giggles and a dog's whimper that was quickly stifled as if somebody had clapped a hand round his muzzle.

'Dave!' murmured Pete. 'He's late – and why on earth has he brought the girls?'

'Young Tracey heard me creeping down the stairs,' Dave explained in a whisper as he and his trekking guests joined us. 'She insisted on coming. We couldn't leave Sharron in case she woke and found Tracey missing.'

'Just as well.' Sharron pulled the hood of her anorak over her head. 'If there are three yobbos, as there must have been last night, you're going to need all the help you can get to tackle them.'

I clutched my hockey stick more tightly, trying to gain comfort from its solid weight. The night-riders might well be older and bigger than we were.

'There may be no need to grapple with them,' Pete soothed. 'They'll probably turn tail once they know they've been discovered.'

'I hope you're right.' Tracey's teeth were chattering. 'I feel scared.'

'We've got Glen, remember.' Dave's grip tightened on the sheepdog's collar as we heard footsteps approaching down the lane. 'Ssh! Keep quiet, all of you, and leave this to me.'

Dave advanced with his hand on Glen's collar. The dog gave a low growl and I sensed the hairs on his back stiffen.

'What do you think you're doing?' Dave's challenge was almost lost as two youths pounced out of the darkness and rolled him to the ground.

Pete hurried to help but, before he could reach Dave, another shape rose from the gloom and downed him with a rugby tackle.

'Leave him alone!' Forgetting my fears, I brandished my hockey stick and ran forward.

'You big cowards!' Sharron scolded the youths. Surprisingly brave in this emergency she was close behind me.

The youth, who was sitting on Dave's chest, looked round.

'Girls!' he exclaimed, amazed. 'What's going on?' He had a strong Bristol accent.

'You tell us.' Pete managed to thrust aside his assailant. 'What d'you mean by coming here at night and riding other people's ponies?'

'Ponies?' echoed one of the other youths. 'Are

you off your nut or something? What would we want with riding ponies? We're on a night exercise from the Inner Cities Camp.'

The youth who had been sitting on Dave's chest stood up.

'We thought you were the enemy,' he explained. 'We're in two groups, see. We five . . .' he indicated his friends who clustered round, 'are a commando gang. We're out to raid the camp and the others are trying to stop us.'

'I wouldn't like to be them, then.' Dave picked himself up and rubbed his elbow ruefully. 'You nearly broke my arm.'

'No danger of that, matey.' The youth who had tackled Pete chuckled. 'We use karate, see. Controlled strength. That's what it's all about. We have lessons from a black belt in Bristol. The object is to subdue your opponent without injuring him.'

'You subdued me, right enough.' Pete put out his hand. 'Shake then. No hard feelings.'

One of the other youths bent to pat Glen who had been sniffing him, no doubt puzzled by the sudden switch to friendliness all round. 'What's all this about night-riding?' the youth asked. 'Has somebody been borrowing your gees?'

'Too right.' Dave explained what had happened the previous night. 'We were waiting to warn off the vandals.'

'We thought you were the night-riders,' added Sharron.

The youth who had been sitting on Dave and who seemed to be the leader of the group looked at the illuminated dial of his watch.

'Half-past three,' he said. 'It'll be starting to get light in an hour. We'll wait with you till then.'

'Would you really?' I was grateful that we would not have to tackle the real night-riders on our own. 'But what about the exercise? Won't the others wonder where you've got to?'

'Do them good to wait a bit.' The youth chuckled. 'They'll think it's part of the strategy, that's all.'

He produced a packet of peanuts and handed them round. Sharron brought out a bag of sweets and we settled down to munch companionably as we kept watch.

From time to time we talked quietly. The group's leader told us that his name was Darren Bates. 'Not that anyone ever uses it,' he explained lightly. 'You can call me Red. Everyone else does. You'll see why when it's daylight.'

The other youths introduced themselves as Terry, Joe, Greg and Woody. Then we fell silent.

The night grew colder and rain began to fall, softly at first and then in heavy, slanting sheets. We huddled beneath the trees.

'This is no use,' Pete decided at last. 'They won't come now. We'd better pack it in. Thanks for your help, chaps.'

'Don't mention it,' said Red. 'It's all part of the adventure camp training.'

'See you again, sometime.' Terry pulled tight the draw-strings of his waterproof jacket. 'We're heading for the cliffs.'

'Us, too.' Pete put out a hand to steer me down the lane.

Tracey began to shiver and Dave put an arm

around her shoulders. 'Come on.' He turned to Sharron. 'Make for the house as quietly as you can. Then put your things to dry on the radiator. We don't want your Mum suspecting you've been out on a night like this.'

When we reached our cottage, Pete and I bade the youths good-bye.

From the stable came the sound of Magic moving sleepily amid her straw.

I cast a glance towards the field but it was still too dark to see Hero drowsing as he should have been beneath the wind-sheared hawthorn. Too wet to go to look for him, Pete and I took off our sodden training shoes in the porch. Holding them in our hands we crept through the kitchen and draped our wet duffle coats in front of the Aga.

At every squeak of the stairs we expected Mummy or Daddy to come out on to the landing to investigate, but they must have been sleeping soundly and we reached our rooms safely. Luckily, although it was Easter, the weather had been cold and so the storage heaters were on. I peeled off my wet cords and jersey and put them over a chair to dry.

I was so tired that I don't even remember getting into bed. I must have fallen heavily asleep because the next thing I knew was Mummy shaking me awake.

'Come on, Pippa. Whatever's wrong with you? I've called you twice already. It's almost half past eight.'

'Oh, dear! And Magic's still in her stable!' Alert now, I reached for my cords and sweater.

'No, you don't.' Mummy took my still-damp

garments from me. 'What were you and Pete doing? I found your coats in front of the Aga. Now these clothes feel wet. It didn't rain until after nightfall. You twins have got some explaining to do. But that will wait until later. For the moment, Pippa, into the bathroom with you and see you have a proper wash. Pulling on any old clothes over your pyjamas and rushing out to the ponies simply won't do.'

'But, Mummy, I've got to see to Magic,' I protested. 'It's time she was let out to graze.'

'Pete's gone out to her,' said my mother. 'He wasn't as tired as you.'

I collected my sponge-bag and made for the bathroom. Before I reached it, however, Pete's voice rose from the garden. For once he sounded distraught.

'Mummy! Pippa! Come quickly! Hero's missing!'

# 7

## 'Phone the police!'

'So now Hero's got out? That pony's a menace!' I exclaimed as Pete came pounding upstairs.

Grumpy from lack of sleep and shivery from two wettings in less than forty-eight hours, I was ready to blame the black for just about everything. 'I hope he hasn't broken down any of the hedges.'

'The hedges are all sound and the gate's still padlocked,' Pete rejoined. 'Hero's saddle and bridle have gone, though. It must have been the night-riders again. They must have come over the fields and taken him while we were keeping guard on the trekking ponies.'

'Somehow they must have undone the padlock and then fastened it,' I puzzled.

'Or jumped Hero out of the field,' said my brother. 'They may be better riders than we thought. Anyway, Hero's missing. That's the problem.'

'Probably the yobbos didn't dare to risk bringing him back in case they were heard.' I tried to sound calm. 'Don't worry too much, Pete. After they'd had their fun they may just have turned him loose.'

I dragged a pair of jeans and a dry sweater from a drawer and, ignoring Mummy's protests, started to dress. 'Wait while I get Magic,' I called after

Pete who was now half-way down the stairs. 'Then you can bring your bike and we'll scour the roads together.'

'I'm phoning the police first,' he said. 'I think Hero's been stolen.'

While Pete reported the missing pony I stifled Mummy's protests by going into the bathroom to wash. Then, waving aside her warning about missing breakfast, I put a couple of chocolate wafers in my pocket and joined Pete outside.

'I phoned Dave as well as the police.' Pete pinged his bicycle bell impatiently while I was saddling Magic. 'There's been a most frightful row at the farm.'

'Oh, dear!' I groaned. 'What happened?'

'Apparently Mrs Garland heard Dave and the girls getting in last night. She was furious with Dave, said he'd betrayed their guests' trust in letting Sharron and Tracey take part in such an irresponsible adventure. Anyway, Tracey's got a temperature this morning which means she can't take part in any search.'

'What about Dave and Sharron?' I asked. 'Are Mrs Garland and the girls' parents letting them come?'

'Dave wasn't sure.' Pete looked doubtful. He stood by Magic's head while I mounted. 'He said that, if they were able to come, they'd meet us at the end of the lane.'

'We'll soon know.' I trotted Magic over the rutted ground while Pete wobbled alongside.

Standing on his pedals, my brother breasted the hill ahead of us. Then he sat down and raised his handlebars in a triumphant 'wheelie' as he rounded the bend at the top.

'They're there,' he reported, 'and they've got Pippin saddled and bridled for me.'

Glen fussed to meet us as we neared the farm gate. Pete wheeled his bicycle into the yard and propped it against a disused horse-rake while Sharron, Dave and I exchanged rueful greetings. Then Pete mounted Pippin and the search was on.

Splitting into twos we covered the main road for twenty minutes or so in each direction. We investigated the side lanes and farm tracks before riding back to report to each other that we'd had no sighting of the missing Hero.

'He wouldn't have wandered further than that in the time.' Dave rubbed his chin thoughtfully as we conferred. 'And Dad phoned round to the neighbouring farms before we started without any luck. I reckon that means that whoever took Hero still has him.'

'Whoever it was probably jumped him out of the field and made off over the cliffs,' said Pete.

'Some rider!' I added with grudging admiration, knowing how difficult the black pony could be.

'What now?' puzzled Dave.

'Why not ride back to the field and see if we can find any tracks?' I suggested. 'After all the heavy rain last night we should find some trace of Hero.'

'Good idea.' Pete turned Pippin into the lane. 'We ought to have tried it earlier.'

'I suppose so,' Sharron agreed. 'As it is we've probably wasted nearly a couple of hours scouring the lanes.'

We halted at the cottage to let Mummy know we'd had no success. Then Pete and Dave went into the field to look for clues while Sharron and I helped Mummy prepare some food for the afternoon's search.

'Luckily I've got some rolls.' Mummy produced polythene bags and a packet of cheese portions. 'If you take these it will be quicker than cutting sandwiches. Then there's the fruit cake I baked yesterday. That and some apples should keep you going.'

I found Pete's rucksack and Sharron helped me pack in the food. Almost before we had finished we heard a shout from Dave and, next moment, Pete ran from the field and burst into the kitchen.

'You were right, Pippa.' He thumped me on the back. 'We've found the place where Hero jumped out. With the ground being so wet, his hoof-marks show where he took off. But it doesn't look as though whoever was riding him made for the cliff path. The tracks point in quite the opposite direction. It looks almost as if they were heading towards the town.'

'Past the old aerodrome, in fact,' I nodded. 'That would be a good place to hide a stolen pony.'

'Yes, in one of the hangars.' Pete slipped on his rucksack. 'Come on. Let's go!'

Prints of a galloping pony showed clear cut in the grass of the field on the other side of the hedge. We followed them to the lane and then Dave spotted black horse hairs on a flattened part of the hawthorn.

'Through here,' he called, holding open the field-gate for the rest of us.

'It looks as if you're right again, Pippa.' Relief was making my brother more cheerful now. 'The thief has taken the shortest route to the aerodrome, sure enough.'

At the far side of the field the tracks ended.

'The wretch probably reined up here for a breather and then went on at a walk,' Dave deduced. 'The ground wasn't really wet enough for Hero's hooves to have cut in unless he was going at quite a fast pace.'

Later we came on a very wet patch in the green lane leading to the old aerodrome and, sure enough, pony hoof-marks showed us that we were on the right trail.

At the aerodrome, however, we drew a blank. Although the great doors of the three war-time hangars were barred, there were enough gaps in the joints of the corrugated iron sheeting for us to peer into the dim interiors. There was enough light, too, for us to have seen any pony that might be within; even a black pony like Hero.

As we turned away from the last of the hangars Pete gave a heavy sigh. 'We must have been wrong after all.'

'But we know the thief brought Hero in this direction,' said Sharron. She gazed round at the landscape. 'Is there anywhere else a pony could have been hidden?'

# 8

## We need help

We gazed hopelessly round at the ponyless land-scape.

'To begin with,' said Dave, 'there are about twenty farms in this area.'

'Not to mention all their outbuildings and barns,' added Pete. 'Searching for Hero is like looking for popcorn on a pebbly beach.'

'Hopeless for the four of us,' I sighed. 'We need help.'

'Pete did notify the police,' Sharron pointed out. 'But they've got quite enough to do looking for lost children, tracing runaway teenagers and controlling football crowds,' I said, 'not to mention dealing with burglars, vandalism and hunting down criminals. Of course, the police'll keep their eyes open for Hero, but we can't expect them to divert the whole of the local force to make a full-scale search.'

Dave straightened Cloud's mane thoughtfully. 'Maybe the Inner Cities Camp could help.'

'Brilliant idea.' Pete looked happier. 'P'raps your Dad could phone up the warden, Dave. If all the campers are like the five commando raiders we met last night I reckon they'd mount an efficient search.'

'There's a phone box just down the lane.' Dave felt in his pocket. 'If we can raise a tenpenny piece between us, I'll ring Dad from there.'

Pete produced a coin and we jogged to the phone box. Dave went inside and the rest of us dismounted to let the ponies graze the roadside verge.

While we were waiting, a cream Mercedes rounded the bend on its wrong side, blaring its horn.

Panicked by the sudden noise, Magic threw up her head and began to prance. Taken by surprise, I lost my grip on her bridle. Pete, holding both Pippin and Cloud, was unable to help while Sharron, at the end of Russet's reins, seemed rooted to the spot.

Magic backed towards the hedge and Sharron, thinking only of avoiding my pony's hooves, dropped Russet's reins and ducked across the road.

The Mercedes pulled up with a squeal of brakes. Both doors opened and three young men came running to our aid.

The tallest, with tousled, dark hair and wearing a quilted green body-warmer over a canary-yellow roll-top jersey, grasped Magic's cheek-piece in a knowledgeable way and talked her to a quivering halt. At the same time, one of the others grabbed Russet. He looked not much older than Dave and was slightly built with gingery sleeked-down hair and a thick Fair Isle sweater.

Meanwhile Cloud was pulling at her reins in order to investigate the third newcomer – a jokey-looking, undersized young man with a clown's face, dark eyes, pasty complexion and straggly blond hair.

He laughed as Cloud nosed the pocket of his leather bomber jacket. 'You know where the sugar's kept, don't you, old girl?' He turned to Pete. 'The mare must have smelled it out. I always keep a few lumps on me.' He held out the sugar on the palm of his hand for Cloud to lip up. 'A bit of sweet stuff comes in handy when you're dealing with horses.'

'You really are horsy, then, are you?' Sharron asked. 'What fun!'

The comic-looking young man seemed to consider. 'Horsy? Yes, I suppose I am. It's my job.'

'How come?' Pete sized him up with interest. 'Are you a jockey? You're about the build.'

'In a manner of speaking, you could say that.' The jokey-looking young man seemed to grow with importance. Then, with a sidelong glance at his companions, he sighed. 'I'd best come clean and admit it. I'm only a stable lad.' He jerked his head towards the youth in the Fair Isle sweater. 'Ginger's the jockey. He's an apprentice, anyway.'

'And what about you?' Sharron turned to the young man in the quilted green body-warmer. 'Are you horsy, too?'

'Horsy enough.' He looked round from fondling Magic to smile indulgently at Sharron. 'You could say I study form at any rate.'

'He studies it well enough to be able to run that Mercedes,' Ginger confirmed. 'He's had some big wins lately, haven't you, Chas?'

'With a little help from his friends,' the jokey youth put in and, for a moment, his face seemed to sharpen with envy. Next second, he resumed his bantering manner. 'Chas is generous, though, aren't you, Charley? Don't mind sharing your good luck with the rest of us, do you?'

'So you're all interested in horses,' I angled. 'I mean you'd know if you'd seen a jet black blood pony, wouldn't you?'

'Course,' nodded Ginger. 'We'd all notice anything special in the way of horseflesh.'

'Then have you seen Hero?' Pete asked. 'He's a potential eventer. I was looking after him for a friend and he's gone missing.'

'Might have been stolen,' added Dave.

'Too bad.' Chas shook his tousled dark head. ''Fraid we haven't seen any pony of that description.'

'You're right though,' broke in Ginger. 'We'd have noticed him if we had.'

'Sounds as if we'd have to be blind to have missed him.' The jokey youth pushed away Cloud who was still nosing his pockets and gave a good-natured smile. 'Tell you what,' he offered. 'We'll keep a good look out from now on. Where can we get in touch with you if we see him?'

The young man called Chas wrote down our telephone numbers in a pocket diary. Then they all three got back into the Mercedes and drove away.

'Mind how you go!' Dave called a warning. 'You never know how many more ponies you're likely to meet down these twisting lanes.'

Sharron glanced at her watch and put a foot in Russet's stirrup. 'It's nearly five o'clock,' she announced with a glance at Dave. 'Time we were getting back or there'll be another panic.'

'You're right.' Dave turned Cloud's head for home. 'Sorry, Pete. We'll meet tomorrow morning for another search.'

'Unless Hero's turned up, meanwhile.' I picked up my reins about to trot after them but Pete pulled me up short.

'Hero won't turn up at the cottage, Pippa. He hasn't been with us long enough to look on it as home but I'll tell you where he might have gone . . .'

'To his own home, Mark's place?' I followed his line of thought. 'Why ever didn't we think of that before? We can't go there now, though, Pete – not to Brampton, it's too late. Mummy and Daddy are easy-going but even they're going to panic if we're not back by six, especially after last night. Can't we just phone?'

'There won't be anybody at Mark's to answer,' Pete reminded me briefly. 'They've all gone to Greece.' He handed me Pippin's reins before feeling in his anorak pocket for another tenpenny piece. 'We're half-way to Brampton as it is, Pippa, so we may as well go on. I'll phone Mum and tell her not to wait supper.' .

After having been up for so long the previous night and then spending most of the day in the saddle, I was half-asleep by the time we reached Brampton. I was jerked awake, however, by the sight of a police car standing in the drive of Linden Lodge, the large house where Mark and his mother lived. Beside it was a yellow sports car and a sober-looking grey Audi.

Pete and I reined up in astonishment. Then, almost before we had recovered from our surprise, a blonde-haired youngish-looking woman, in an expensive fur jacket, hurried down the steps from the front door and ran across the gravel towards us. Behind her came a police constable and a man of about forty in a well-cut, grey suit.

'You must be friends of Mark's,' the woman greeted us. 'I'm his mother. Please tell me if you've seen him. All I want is for him to come back home.'

# 9

## The mystery deepens

My brother stared at Mrs Cooper in bewilderment.

'I thought Mark was with you,' he said blankly 'I thought you were all holidaying in Greece.'

'So we should have been.' The grey-suited man removed his thin-rimmed spectacles and wiped them with a spotless handkerchief. 'We'd all have been on Mykonos by now if your friend hadn't taken it into his head to run away.'

'Run away?' I echoed. 'Why would Mark have done that?'

'It's beyond my understanding.' The man looked exasperated. 'Any boy would have given his right arm to spend three weeks on a Greek island.'

'It may depend on the boy.' Pete looked uncomfortable.

'But you've had some news of Mark haven't you?' Mrs Cooper looked from one to the other of us eagerly. 'That must be why you've come.'

''Fraid not.' Pete shook his head. Then he plucked at Pippin's mane in embarrassment. 'Pippa and I came here to see if Hero had turned up. That's all.'

'Hero?' The man looked sharply at Pete. 'Don't say the pony's missing too. A valuable animal like that! I said Mark was foolish to leave him with a school-friend.' He gazed at Pete accusingly. 'Now I suppose you've let the pony get out. I hope he doesn't cause any damage. Allowing an animal to stray on the highway is an offence. That could incur a heavy fine.'

'Douglas! For goodness' sake, stop being so legal-minded!' Mark's mother was near tears. 'Mark's missing. He's been unhappy enough to run away – and all you can think about is the penalty for straying animals.'

'Hero may not have strayed,' Pete pointed out. 'He could have been stolen.'

'Stolen?' the man echoed, and I knew now who Mark's stepfather-to-be was – Douglas Finch, the well-known local solicitor who, according to Daddy, was 'mustard' when it came to acting for the police in prosecuting erring motorists. 'This gets worse.' He glanced towards the constable who was standing stolidly by. 'I suppose you've notified the theft?'

'Of course.' I came to Pete's defence. 'That was the first thing Pete did when he realised Hero was missing. The pony couldn't just have strayed, you see. All our fences are good. You can't blame Pete, Mr Finch. He's taken the responsibility of looking after Hero very seriously. He hasn't had a moment's peace since we found the pony missing. We've been searching all day.'

Douglas Finch repolished his spectacles before turning to Mark's mother. 'You see now, Norma, how right I was to arrange for Hero to be sold. For a boy of Mark's age to own such a valuable animal can lead to endless problems.'

Pete looked the man straight in the eyes. 'Mark's

51

father gave him Hero, Mr Finch. I wouldn't have thought he was anyone else's to sell.'

The solicitor looked taken aback. 'You're being impertinent,' he retorted. 'If you're a sample of Mark's friends, then the sooner he's sent away to public school the better.'

'Oh, be quiet, Douglas. The important thing is to find Mark.' Mrs Cooper looked from the man she was intending to marry to Pete. 'Surely you've some idea where he might be?'

'Not a clue,' said Pete. His lips moved silently and I knew his thoughts. If Mrs Cooper was intending to let Douglas Finch take charge of Mark's destiny then Pete wouldn't have given away his friend's whereabouts even if he'd known them.

\*　　\*　　\*　　\*

'I think Mrs Cooper's making a big mistake in marrying that stuffed shirt,' Pete declared as we rode home. 'I wonder what on earth she can see in him. He's very different from Mark's Dad. He plays rugby and sails while that Finch is as dry as the dust on his law books. And he seems mean too. Did you notice? What really upset him was that Hero was such an expensive pony. He wasn't at all worried that Hero might be ill-treated or in danger. Mrs Cooper must be off her chump to think of marrying him. It quite surprised me the way she stood up to him.'

It had surprised me, too, but then grown-up behaviour often did.

'Mrs Cooper looked quite an expensive sort of lady.' I thought of the silver-fox jacket she had been wearing. 'And Mark's real father sounds the sort of man who puts sport first and is often changing his job. Perhaps Mrs Cooper felt she wanted more security.'

'Mark's Dad hasn't changed his job all that often,' defended Pete. 'He's always been in engineering. It's just that his line has varied a bit. Mark said his father was a ship's engineer, like our Dad. Then when he got married he came ashore and started a garage. He specialised in racing cars.'

I nodded. 'He would. He sounds just that sort of man. What Daddy would call a man's man. Nice enough, but perhaps that wasn't what Mark's Mum wanted.'

Falling silent, I patted Magic's neck. How lucky we were, Pete and I, that our parents seemed more or less contented with each other. It would be difficult to imagine them ever splitting up.

As so often happened, Pete picked up the line of my thoughts.

'It's bad luck for Mark not to be part of a proper family,' said Pete. 'No wonder his Dad bought him Hero to compensate.'

I nodded. As Cliff Cottage came into view, I nudged Magic to a faster trot.

'Mark's father must have felt he had a lot to make up to Mark,' Pete went on. 'With his father gone and Mr Finch taking over and bossing everything, Mark must feel he's no longer got a real home.'

'But where is Mark?' I puzzled. 'And why's he gone? D'you think he's trying to teach his mother a lesson? Or can he be trying to join his father in the Gulf?'

'Out of the question, I'd say.' Pete was definite.

'He probably doesn't have a separate passport and, even if he did, the fare would cost too much. No. I know exactly what Mark's doing – just what I'd have done in his place.'

'What's that?' Reining up outside the cottage gate, I slid from the saddle and pulled my pony's reins over her head ready to lead her to the stable.

'He's taken Hero, of course.' Pete dismounted beside me. 'He had to.' His voice was muffled by the saddle-flap as he unbuckled Pippin's girth. 'Otherwise Mr Finch would have had the pony collected from us and taken away to be sold.'

'Beastly man!'

Pete looped Pippin's reins beneath the fence and secured them with a slip-knot.

'Let's leave the ponies here for now. There's no point in making Mum wait any longer. She'll have kept our supper hot for hours as it is.'

I was about to protest that we ought to see to the ponies before we thought of eating but the cottage door opened and Mummy looked out.

'Oh, good!' she exclaimed. 'I thought I heard you two. The telephone's kept ringing and a young man's been asking for Pete.'

'Best come indoors, son, in case he rings again.' Daddy's voice floated from above the seven o'clock news. 'I asked the lad whether he was ringing about Hero but each time he just rang off.'

Pete and I exchanged glances.

'It could have been Mark,' I said.

'Mark?' Mummy queried quickly. 'I thought he was supposed to be in Greece and that was why you were looking after Hero.'

Before I could say anything Pete gave me a

warning glance.

'That's right, Mum,' he confirmed. 'Pippa's raving. Mark and his people should have left the day before yesterday. Tell you what, Pippa,' he said meaningfully, 'why don't you take Pippin to the stable with Magic and give them both a feed? They get on well enough together. Meanwhile I'll give Dave a ring and ask him if it will be O.K. if we take Pippin back to the farm in the morning.'

Dad came out of the sitting room and picked up his coastguard's cap from the hall table. 'I'm standing watch tonight but I'm a bit early. I'll have time to take Pippin up to the farm before I go to the coastguard station. It's not much out of my way.' He gave Magic a friendly pat before untying Pippin's reins. 'You see to your own pony, now, Pippa. The shepherd's pie has been in the bottom oven so long it won't hurt for another twenty minutes.' He gave Pete a hard stare. 'You want to keep the line open in case your friend phones again. And, remember, if it's news of Hero don't go taking any foolish action on your own. Remember you've got a responsibility to Mark's parents, as well as to him.'

'Whatever made Daddy say that?' I wondered aloud as Pete and I were washing up the dishes after supper. 'Do you think he suspects anything?'

'How could he?' Pete gave an extra hard polish to the plate he was holding. 'Dad and Mum still think Mark's in Greece. We'd better keep it that way,' he decided. 'In view of Douglas Finch's behaviour in wanting to sell Hero, I think our loyalty is to Mark and his real father. Don't you agree, twin?'

# 10

## A message from Mark

'It seems Mark's not going to ring again, after all,' I sighed.

Pete and I were on our way to pay Magic a goodnight visit.

'Perhaps he's scared of using the phone box, again,' my brother said. 'What with all the boys from the Inner Cities Camp looking for Hero, Mark might have felt he was in danger of being spotted.'

'And now the police are looking for him, too.' I patted Magic's neck as she crunched a piece of carrot. 'Well, at least we know now that Hero's most likely with Mark and that he hasn't been stolen by a bunch of night-riding hooligans.'

'That's true.' Pete fingered the padlock on the stable door. 'But it wasn't Mark who rode Cloud and the trekking ponies the other night. Those yobbos might still decide to pay us another visit.' He drew me away from the door and snapped home the padlock. 'Well, at least we can make sure they don't ride Magic.'

It didn't seem as though the night-riders had visited any of the ponies because Dave was on the telephone next morning, before we'd finished breakfast, to discuss plans for the day and he told us that nothing untoward had happened at the farm.

'Good!' Pete said into the mouthpiece. 'I heard Glen bark a couple of times during the night. I wondered whether I ought to get up and investigate but then I thought you'd probably have heard the barking, too, and, before I could make up my mind, I must have dropped off to sleep.'

I heard Dave chuckle at the other end and put my ear near Pete's to hear him say: 'Same here. I s'pose we were all dog tired after all the riding. What time do we start this morning? I take it the search is still on.'

'Sort of.' Pete looked round to see if he was being overheard. Then, as Mummy came into the room with the eggs and bacon, he said quickly, 'See you up at the farm in about an hour, Dave. We'll decide the route later.'

'I hope you two aren't going to wear yourselves out, looking for that pony.' Mummy sat down and began to pour the coffee. 'Hero'll turn up, either here or at the Coopers', when he's tired of freedom.'

I wolfed down my toast and the last of my egg, gulped half a cup of coffee and dashed out to see to Magic.

'Wait for me, Pippa,' called Pete. 'I'll give you a hand. You get Magic's feed while I muck out. Dave's expecting us at the farm at nine. If we don't want to give the show away about Mark running off, we'll at least have to go through the motions of looking for Hero.' He dashed past me and then paused. 'Have you got the key to Magic's padlock?'

'I'll unlock it.' I sped past my brother to the door

and then stopped short. Something seemed to be stuck through the hasp – a rolled-up piece of paper. Was it a note?

Pete straightened it out. 'It's from Mark. Listen to this:

"Where were you yesterday? I kept phoning and your mother said you were out. The last time I tried to ring I was nearly spotted by a policeman on a motor-bike. You'll know by now that I've run away. I've got Hero, too, so don't worry about him. I'll tell you all about it when I see you. Meanwhile can you ride to Two Crosses to meet me at mid-day? There's a barn in the field beside the Pack Horse Bridge." '

'We'd better take some provisions,' I said.

'But how?' Pete looked thoughtful.

'Mummy's going to the Garlands' after she's washed up,' I told him. 'I heard her telling Dad that she and Mrs Garland were going to pick catkins to put with the daffodils for the W.I. flower-arranging class this afternoon. That'll keep them busy for most of the morning.'

'Which gives us a chance to raid the larder on Mark's behalf,' said Pete.

'But should we?' I wavered. 'Won't it be like stealing?'

'Not from our own home,' Pete said. 'Besides it's an emergency. We can't let Mark starve.'

'Perhaps we can keep an account of what we take,' I suggested. 'Then we can tell Mummy about it later.'

'And offer to make up the provisions from our pocket money.' My brother thumped my shoulder. 'Good thinking, Pippa.'

While I was grooming Magic I saw Mummy set off for the farm. So, leaving one side unbrushed, I stuffed some hay into a net and left Magic to pull at it while I foraged for provisions.

Pete filled his rucksack with pony nuts for Hero while I went to the cottage to pack a haversack for Mark.

I put on two eggs to hard-boil. Then I took half a loaf from the batch that Mummy had baked yesterday. I cut some cheese, two slices of ham and a slice of cold beef before adding four rock buns, a couple of apples and a packet of digestive biscuits.

'That should keep Mark going for twenty-four hours,' I told Pete as I reported back to the stable. 'Then, when I looked at so much food left in the larder, I thought Mummy might not even notice anything had gone.'

'That's one good thing about being in a farm-house – super-stocked larder.' My brother glanced at the bulging haversack. 'Imagine what a hole that would have left in the larder of our Dormville semi.'

At the Garlands', Dave was waiting with Cloud. Tracey had recovered from her previous day's chill. She and her sister were already mounted on the trekking ponies and riding them round the home field over a low pole which Dave had set up to introduce them to jumping.

'Sorry we can't offer you a mount, Pete.' Dave jerked his head towards the Exmoors. 'As you can see, both Pippin and Russet are spoken for. Good thing you've brought your bike. You'll be able to make enquiries at houses along the road while the rest of us cover the farms and outbuildings.'

'Actually, the search is off.' Pete told Dave about Mark's note. 'Pippa and I are on our way to Two Crosses now to take him provisions.' He glanced over at Sharron and Tracey who were now trotting towards us. 'Do you think we can trust the girls?'

'Of course,' I said quickly. 'Especially if we explain that Mr Finch was intending to get Mark off the scene, in Greece, and then sell Hero.'

'We're with you all the way,' Sharron declared, after listening carefully to what Pete had to say. 'Mark's stepfather-to-be sounds a real horror.'

\*     \*     \*     \*

It was a pleasant ride to Two Crosses. The ponies trotted briskly, enjoying the fresh, morning air. I rode with Sharron, and Dave rode beside Tracey while Pete pedalled just behind.

Magic seemed to benefit from the trekking ponies' sensible company. There was no dancing sideways, no frothing her bit or shying at shadows. My pony was again the sensible mare she had been before Hero's arrival. It seemed my training really was effective and that entering her for the Novice Dressage Test might be a definite possibility.

I halted her at the next crossroads and reined my pony back a few steps just for practice.

'Magic's really coming on,' Dave admired.

We clattered through Two Crosses hamlet, past the swinging inn-sign, the couple of rose-embowered cottages and on towards the Pack Horse Bridge.

Then, as we rounded the bend before the bridge, we saw a commotion ahead of us. A band of youths in the green denims and guernseys of the Inner Cities Camp were beating on the tarmac with their sticks and shouting raucous encouragement to five of their number who were running across the field towards a stone-built barn.

'Mark!' gasped Pete in alarm. 'Somehow those chaps must have picked up his trail.' He stood on his pedals to ride faster, calling to the youths to lay off as he rode.

'Best head them off.' Dave turned Cloud on to the verge and trotted her to the field-gate. 'Darn the thing!' He leant down to tug at the metal. 'It's stuck in the mud.'

'Keep clear, Dave,' I warned. 'Come on, Magic!'

I set my pony at the wall. Taken by surprise, Magic's take-off was short.

'Up, girl!'

Could she do it? Leaning forward I lifted her head with my reins. I heard a ring of iron as Magic's hooves caught the top stones of the wall.

Next moment I was flying through the air. After that, I knew no more.

# 11

'Is that really you?'

'Are you all right, Pippa? Oh, please say something!'

Sharron's face swam into focus as I came to my senses a few moments later.

I raised my head gingerly. 'I think so.'

The world had stopped spinning so I sat up. My shoulder hurt but I could move my arm. So I hadn't broken my collar-bone.

Dave was standing beside my pony who was trailing a broken girth.

'Magic went head over heels,' explained Tracey. 'And so did you.'

Suddenly it all came back to me – the crazy jump I had attempted and why. I glanced across the field to the barn. The boys from the Inner Cities Camp were still surging across the field while Pete stood hesitating, half-way, torn between the need to intercept the lads before they found Mark and the desire to see if I was in one piece.

'I'm O.K., Pete,' I groaned, collecting my scattered senses. 'Call off the pack.'

Too late!

Before Pete could intervene, Red Bates, the leader of the five youths, reached the barn. At the same time the heavy door burst open. Red was knocked backwards and I glimpsed a dark-haired boy of about Pete's age vaulting into the saddle of a black pony – it was Mark and Hero!

My heart was in my mouth as one of the other boys grabbed at Hero's reins. He missed but managed to grasp the nearside stirrup leather.

Mark pushed him away with his heel, whipped Hero round and set off at a gallop – irons flying, the black pony's tail pluming as they went.

'Go on, you lot,' Red called to Dave, Sharron and me. 'You've got ponies. Give chase!'

'The hunt's off.' Pete began to explain as I took Magic's reins from Dave and walked shakily across the field with the others.

'Hero's not been stolen, after all,' Tracey added, trotting Pippin towards the youths.

'Who's that making off with him, then?' Red demanded, dusting himself down.

'His owner – Mark Cooper.' Shame-faced Pete kicked at a tuft of grass. 'The whole thing's been a mistake.'

'Stone the crows!' said Greg. 'Mistake, is it? And us out half the night and all this morning, looking for him!' He rounded on Pete. 'You've got some explaining to do, mate.'

'I have,' admitted my brother, 'and I will.'

The youths listened while Pete told them how Mark had been driven to make off with Hero to prevent Mr Finch selling him.

'Poor kid,' said Greg at last. 'So life isn't all plain sailing, even for a well-heeled youngster like that.'

'What do we do now, then?' wondered Joe. 'Call off the search?' He gestured towards the rest of the boys from the camp who were still clustered in the road. 'Come here, you lot!'

'Steady!' cautioned Red. He turned to Pete. 'You can't trust all of them like you can trust us five and you don't want to risk the Camp Warden getting to know your pal's whereabouts. He'd feel it was his duty to grass to the fuzz. O.K.?'

'You're right,' Pete nodded as the rest of the Inner Cities campers pounded across the field towards us.

'What's this, then?' A long-haired seventeen-year-old, who seemed to be their self-appointed leader, sounded aggressive. 'How come you let them get away?' He glared from Dave to Pete before glancing scornfully at Sharron, Tracey and me. 'Call yourselves riders! You ought to be half-way across Exmoor, on the trail, by now.'

'Yeh!' A blank-faced lad who was growing out a skinhead haircut grabbed at Cloud's bridle and challenged Dave. 'If you can't cope, hand over the nag to me.'

'Lay off, Chalky.' Red knocked off the lad's outstretched hand, jerking his head towards me. 'Didn't you see the girl fall? That's what caused the hold-up.'

'That's right,' said Pete. He put out a hand to steady me and I suddenly realised how wobbly I felt.

'Besides,' Sharron pointed to Magic, 'her pony's burst its girths. No one could ride far with that saddle.'

'I don't think I could ride at all.' I put my arm over Magic's outstretched neck and felt comforted by the way my pony nuzzled against me. 'I'll have to lead her home.'

'Too far,' said Dave. He handed over Cloud's reins to Sharron. 'Can you lead the mare? She's very quiet. I'm taking Pippa home by bus. There's one due outside the pub in about ten minutes.'

Meanwhile Pete had been securing my pony's girths with string.

'Don't worry about Magic, Pippa. I'll lead her from my bike.'

'What about us, then?' The long-haired boy turned to Red. 'Surely we're not going to call the whole thing off and let the thief get away with the pony, just like that?'

'Not likely! I've got an idea.' Red turned to give Pete a quick wink before gesturing to the remainder of the youths to gather round. 'That fellow rode off in the direction of Little Minton. Now if we hare after him we'll only scare him off further. The best thing is for us to go back to the camp, get our lunch and then ask the Warden to organise transport to take us over to the Little Minton area this afternoon.'

'Suits me.' Chalky slumped down on a clump of heather. He broke off a piece of chocolate and put it into his mouth. 'I'm bushed. Tell you what, Reddo – why not phone the warden from the kiosk by the bridge and get them to bring the truck over here for us now? That way we might just have enough strength left to have another search.'

\*　　\*　　\*　　\*

'Don't make too much of my fall,' I warned Dave as we neared the cottage. 'If Mummy knows I was knocked out, even for a few seconds, she'll say I've

65

been concussed and insist on getting the doctor.'

'And so she should,' said Dave.

'I know. But then they wouldn't let me ride for days — and Mark may need us. Please don't say anything to Mummy,' I begged. 'I promise I'll be careful. I'm not an idiot.'

Even so, I had to promise to rest all afternoon before Mummy would agree to go off with Dave's mother to the W.I.

Pete hitched a lift in Mrs Garland's car so that he could take Magic's girth to the saddler's to be mended and to pick up a spare.

Still feeling shaky, I lay on the sitting-room sofa with a rug over me and looked through a pile of old pony magazines.

My head still ached and I was only half-way through an article on dressage when I decided to give up. I lay back and closed my eyes. I must have dropped off to sleep because I woke with a jerk to hear the phone ringing.

'Woodley, Cliff Cottage,' I said into the mouth-piece.

A clicking sound told me that the caller was in a public call-box. Then came a boy's voice.

'Can I speak to Pete?'

'I'm afraid he's out. Who wants him?'

'Who're you?' the caller hedged.

'I'm Pete's sister, Pippa.' In spite of my aching head I had a sudden intuition. 'Is that you, Mark?'

# 12

## Conspirators

There was silence at the other end of the line. I dreaded that the unknown caller might ring off.

'You can tell me who you are,' I persuaded. 'If you are Mark, I can promise that both Pete and I are on your side. So are all your friends.'

'O.K.' Mark admitted his identity. 'I'll trust you, Pippa. I need friends – but not too many. The more people who know that Hero and I are still in the district, the greater the danger of my future stepfather finding out.'

'You can rely on us.' A desperate note in the boy's voice had made me realise how much he could do with our help. 'You need fodder for Hero and food for yourself. When did you last eat?'

'I took some buns from a baker's van, this morning,' confessed Mark. 'The roundsman was making a delivery so I just grabbed the nearest polythene bagful and left some money.'

'You can't last long on buns.' I told Mark how we had tried to deliver food for him and pony nuts for Hero to the barn by the Pack Horse Bridge. 'The stuff's still packed, if only we can get it to you. Where are you now?'

'Nearer than you think.' In spite of his predicament Mark couldn't resist a chuckle. 'I'm speaking from the kiosk by the bus shelter at the end of your lane. I had to take the risk. I'm desperate.'

'Where's Hero?'

'Safe enough. I've left him hidden.'

'Then why not come to the cottage?' I said. 'Everybody's out but me. Mummy won't be back until half-past four.'

'Won't Pete be back before then?' Mark sounded hesitant.

'No. He's getting a lift with Mummy and Mrs Garland.'

Mark still waited, as if trying to make up his mind, so I went on impulsively: 'It's all right, Mark. I may be only a girl but at least I can hand over the rations. Better still, I can cook you some bacon and eggs. I'll expect you in five minutes.'

Without giving him a chance to argue I put down the phone.

Strangely my headache seemed to have vanished with the excitement. Even my legs seemed to have stopped wobbling as I lifted the hood of the Aga hotplate, cracked a couple of eggs into the frying pan and let them sizzle with two rashers of bacon. I'd put it all to keep hot in the bottom oven and was just frying a couple of rounds of bread when I had a sudden feeling that I was being watched.

Looking round quickly I saw a boy's face at the window. It was a lean clever-looking face, tanned by the open air. The grey eyes were wary, the forehead crowned by dark-brown hair. Mark!

'Come in,' I called. 'It's quite safe and I've made you a lovely meal.'

Mark looked over his shoulder. Then silently – as silently as he must have crept over the shingle of the path – he entered the kitchen.

'Thanks. Where's the pony fodder?'

'In the stable. Pete and I had to put it where Mummy and Daddy wouldn't find it.' With the oven glove I lifted the hot dinner plate to the table and slid the fried bread to join the bacon and eggs. 'I'll fetch the rucksack now. You start on that.'

While Mark ate I made coffee. As he was drinking it I questioned him.

'Where's Hero now?'

'In a barn.' Still cautious, Mark was giving little away.

'The pony must be hungry,' I said.

Above the coffee mug Mark shook his head. 'There were some bales of hay in the barn. Before that I took some mangolds from a sheepfold. Dad will have to do some settling up later.'

'I don't suppose he'll mind.' I looked at Mark closely. 'What are you planning to do? You can't stay hidden for ever.'

'I know. That's why I sent a message to Dad from the Post Office. I asked Dad to get in touch with Mum to tell her Hero belongs to him. When that's established Douglas Finch won't be able to sell the pony.'

'And you'll go back to your Mum?' I suggested.

Mark nodded. 'As long as I can keep Hero, I can put up with anything. I don't mind swotting. I expect I could pass even Douglas Finch's rotten law exams in the end. That's if he still insists on making me into a solicitor. What they don't understand is that I can look after Hero and still have time for my school work.'

'I know,' I sympathised. 'I had the same problem

convincing Mummy about Magic.'

'We haven't time to chat.' Mark gulped down the last of the coffee and fixed on the rucksack. 'It's a pity Pete isn't around. I thought he might have had some useful ideas as to where I could keep Hero for the next few days.'

'There's only one place,' I said. 'Pete would tell you the same.' I thought back to the picnic ride we'd had with Dave and the girls on the afternoon of Hero's arrival. 'There's a barn in a gully a little way back from the Hidden Cove. It's covered in ivy and half-hidden by bracken. No one ever goes there. Not many people even know of the Hidden Cove, so you'd both be perfectly safe.'

'The Hidden Cove?' queried Mark. 'I've heard of the place. Where is it?'

I started to explain the route but, before I had finished giving him the directions, I realised Mark was no longer listening. The colour had drained from his face and he seemed to be staring towards the cliff path. I followed his gaze and saw, coming towards the cottage, a stocky man in a reefer and peaked cap. It was my father.

'A coastguard!' Mark glanced around the room, searching for an exit. 'So you betrayed me, Pippa. I might have known I couldn't trust a girl!'

'Don't talk rubbish,' I retorted hotly. 'I didn't know Daddy would be coming home just now. He's supposed to be on duty until six. Anyway,' I jerked my head towards the inner door, 'you can get out that way, through the sitting-room window. Quick, before he spots you!'

Mark darted into the sitting-room and closed the door behind him. I had no time to hide his dirty plate and mug before Daddy came into the kitchen.

'What have you been doing, Pippa?' The smell of bacon obviously teased my father's nostrils and his eyes took in the unwashed dishes. 'I thought you were supposed to be resting. Your mother phoned me at the coastguard station because she was worried about you. I came to see if you were all right. Now I find you've been cooking some kind of meal. Why?'

'I was hungry, Daddy,' I fibbed. 'Falling off Magic made me feel sick at lunch-time so I didn't want anything to eat. Then I had a sleep and I felt better. I fried myself some bacon and egg.'

'Two eggs, by the look of it,' Daddy's gaze fell on the cracked shells still lying on the draining-board. 'Coffee, too. It looks as if your mother had no need to worry about you, after all, Pippa. You've made me feel hungry. How about fixing me a bacon sandwich before I go back on duty? I'll make the coffee. Fancy another cup?'

Dazedly I set about frying another rasher of bacon and slicing a wholemeal roll. Now that the excitement of my encounter with Mark was over, my headache had come back and my legs felt more wobbly than ever.

Daddy watched me in silence for a few moments. Then he took the frying pan from me.

'You look terrible, Pippa.' He pushed me towards the sitting-room. 'Go and lie down. I'll finish off here and bring a cup of coffee to you when I've done.'

Dizzily I sank on to the sofa. I pulled the rug up to my shoulders but I could not stop shivering.

What did Daddy really think? Had he believed my story about cooking myself a meal or did he

71

suspect what had really happened? If so, what would he do?

I wasn't left long in suspense. A few minutes later Daddy came to the sitting-room carrying a tray. He handed me a mug of sweetened coffee and then sat down on the armchair facing me. Balancing the tray on his knee he began to eat his bacon roll.

'I'm not going to ask you any more questions, Pippa,' he said after the first few mouthfuls. 'I don't want you to lie to me. And I don't want you to volunteer anything either. Now think hard. You see, anything you tell me, I might have to report. The coastguard service has been alerted, along with the police, to watch out for a missing boy, Mark Cooper, the boy who lent Pete the black pony. Now I don't know whether Mark's likely to come here or not. I don't know if he's already been here. What I do know is that his mother must be off her head with worry about him.'

I had an image of Mrs Cooper's anxious face as it had been the previous evening and my eyes filled with tears.

'Mothers are like that – worriers,' Daddy went on. It was as if he was speaking half to himself. 'Your Mum was almost beside herself just now when she phoned me about you, Pippa. Oh, I know she went off to the W.I. but when she got there she wished she hadn't gone. She felt she shouldn't have left you here on your own. She thought she ought to have got the doctor to give you the once over.'

I bit my lip. 'There's no need, Daddy. I'm all right, really.'

'Maybe you are, provided you keep quiet and

don't have any more excitement. But what about Mark Cooper's mother? If you know he's safe, you ought to let her know.'

I looked miserably at Daddy. Kind and considerate as always, he was showing patience and understanding with me now. I didn't like to defy him but Mark's secret wasn't mine to give away.

'It's not just Mark's Mum who's involved, Daddy,' I said. 'Mark's parents are getting a divorce. Mrs Cooper's going to marry Mr Finch, the solicitor. Mark's father gave him Hero and now Mr Finch wants to sell the pony. Mark tried to reach his dad to tell him about it.'

Daddy listened gravely while I poured out the unhappy problem.

'Mark's keeping Hero hidden only to give his father time to act,' I said. 'If the pony's found before then Mr Finch'll be so angry that he'll get rid of him right away.' I looked at my father pleadingly. 'We can't give Mark away, Daddy. He's got to have more time.'

'Hm!' Daddy downed the last of his coffee and scratched his head. 'It's a problem, Pippa, and no mistake. I can sympathise with Mark all right. Parental squabbles are very hard for young peope to bear. On the other hand, there's Mrs Cooper to be considered, not to mention my duty as a coastguard.'

'Oh, Daddy, please!' I begged. 'Just give Mark and his father a chance.'

Daddy took my empty coffee cup and set it on the tray.

'Twenty-four hours, then, Pippa, and that's the limit.'

# 13

## What should we do?

Daddy being so kind and understanding made me feel worse.

Being torn between sympathy for Mark's mother and the necessity to keep Mark's whereabouts secret did absolutely nothing for my headache.

Round and round Daddy's words chased through my brain: 'Twenty-four hours, then, and that's the limit.'

Meanwhile suppose something untoward happened, something to harm Mark? Would it be our fault for not reporting Mark's visit to the cottage? Would Daddy be blamed – perhaps even lose his job as part-time coastguard?

Should we persuade Mark to give himself up? Perhaps he could strike a bargain with his prospective stepfather that might enable him to keep Hero. The thought of Finch's pale, stern face, his probing, fish-like eyes behind their thin-rimmed spectacles made me realise that he was a man who would not compromise easily.

By far the safest thing would be for Mark to keep Hero well hidden until word came from Mark's father to change the position. I thought that Mark ought to take Hero right away from the area. They could travel by night so as not to be seen. They could be far away by dawn.

We'd have to warn Mark. But how? We didn't really know where Mark and Hero were hiding.

Although I'd suggested to Mark that he should take Hero to the barn in the gully near the Hidden Cove there was no guarantee that he would do so. He might not even trust me. He might have suspected that a few understanding words from Daddy might make me give away the secret of his visit. Yes, Mark would have been right in thinking I might unwittingly betray him. I heard again the bitterness in his voice as he'd said: 'I might have known I couldn't trust a girl!'

Very well! I'd prove him wrong!

Footsteps in the lane alerted me to the fact that Mummy and Pete were back.

Rubbing my cheeks with my hands to give them some colour, I went out to meet them.

'There you are, Pippa.' Mummy was carrying in her driftwood arrangement of daffodils and cat-kins. 'How do you feel, dear?'

'Better, Mummy, thank you. I'm quite O.K. now.' I turned to Pete. 'So you got the new girth. Good. Bring it to the stable. Then you can help me bed down Magic.'

'Can't we leave her in the field until supper time?' Pete groaned. 'I want my tea.'

'You can't have your tea until Mummy's got it, can you?' I looked promptingly at my twin. 'Be a sport, Pete. With pony thieves about, I won't be happy until Magic's safely padlocked in.'

'That's right, dear,' Mummy nodded to him. 'Go along and give Pippa a hand. I don't want her to do much bending or straw forking.' She turned to me, searchingly. 'Are you sure you'll be all right, Pippa? If not, Pete could bed the pony down and give her a feed.'

'I'll manage, Mummy,' I said quickly. 'I'd be glad for Pete to fill the hay net for me but I want to measure the pony nuts myself.'

\* \* \* \*

'What's it all about, then?' Pete turned to face me as soon as we were safely out of earshot. 'Don't tell me you've heard from Mark!'

'Better than that,' I said, 'and, in a way, worse. Mark's been here and Daddy nearly caught him.' Quickly I told Pete all that had taken place.

'We'll have to contact Mark and warn him about Daddy's time limit,' I ended. 'Oh, Pete. I know I'm an idiot, letting Daddy know Mark had been here, but what could I do? He'd half-guessed, anyway, and I felt so guilty.'

'Dad can be very persuasive,' Pete agreed. 'Don't be too hard on yourself, Pippa. You weren't feeling well. The trouble is, though, that it could be disastrous for Mark. You're right about wanting to warn him. He may well have gone to the Hidden Cove, and I think we should go there as soon as possible.'

'Mummy will never let me go,' I sighed. 'Not after my getting that bang on my head. You'll have to borrow Magic, Pete, and ride over yourself.'

'Mum and Dad wouldn't let me go either, not at this time of the evening.' Pete frowned and then his brow cleared. 'Tell you what, though, Pippa. I could wait until they've gone to bed and then go.'

'If you're going tonight, so am I.' I set my jaw determinedly. 'I feel better now, Pete. You can have Magic and I'll ride one of the trekking ponies. They're quiet enough to ride bareback and I can use the old bridle Dave gave us when we had Comet.'

\* \* \* \*

The moon was riding high so we were able to make good speed. Even so, it was nearly one o'clock before we reached Dunkerton Beacon. Then came flat, windswept moorland with clumps of heather and gorse starkly etched in the moonlight. Occasionally our ponies' hoof-beats disturbed a nesting bird. A curlew flew from its eggs with a startled cry and somewhere a vixen screeched.

As we zig-zagged down the cliff path to the beach we heard the liquid-sounding *kleep-kleep* of oyster-catchers on the tide-line. Then we were cantering along the sands to the line of jagged rocks guarding the entrance to Hidden Cove.

It was dark in the narrow, dog-leg passage between the high rocks so we slowed to a walk, slackening our reins to let the ponies pick their own way through the slippery, seaweedy boulders that emerged, half-covered, from the sand.

Once into the cove itself, the moonlight was so bright that it made us blink. We glanced round, taking our bearings from the jetty.

'Over there!' I spotted the gully partly hidden amid the dark shapes of gorse and low thorn bushes.

'Quiet!' Pete warned, dismounting to lead Magic. 'If Mark's there we don't want to startle him.'

We picked our way through the gorse towards the ivy-clad barn.

Suddenly the peace of the night was shattered. Startlingly, a shot exploded above our heads.

'Halt!' called a voice, and in the moonlight three dark-clad figures loomed up to bar our way ahead.

Terrified, I froze – the hand that was holding Russet's bridle was icy near the bit.

My brother was made of sterner stuff.

'Who's there?' Pete challenged. 'And what do you think you're doing, firing at us?'

'Cor! It's those kids,' came a voice and I recognised the slight build of the apprentice jockey, Ginger, whom we had met near the disused aerodrome the other day.

'What are you two doing here at this time of night?' Chas sounded as stern as any other grown-up under the circumstances. He broke open the breech of his gun. 'Sorry if I frightened you but we thought you were poachers.'

'Yes, you might have got a peppering of shot.' Trevor's clown face was serious now. 'What are you up to, anyway?'

'We could ask you the same thing,' Pete parried.

'We've told you,' Chas said blandly. 'We're waiting for poachers.'

'Poachers?' echoed Pete. 'Out here?'

'Yeah! Out here.' Trevor was suddenly hostile. 'Want to make something of it, do you? We've had enough trouble as it is, without taking aggro from school kids.'

'Cool it, Trevor.' Chas rested the butt of his gun on the ground and said calmly: 'Strange though it sounds, we have been troubled with poachers. I rented an old cottage nearby for the holiday. I'd hoped to do a bit of rough shooting, perhaps take a trout or two from the stream – and then, what happens? Poachers. Parties of them, taking the rabbits and deer.'

'Sounds odd,' Pete puzzled. 'Could it be the boys from the Inner Cities Camp? They're on some kind of commando exercise.'

'The lad we found wasn't from any inner cities . . .' began Trevor, to be cut short by Chas.

'I told you to shut it.' The leader of the three no longer sounded quite so smooth. 'Of course he came from the camp.' Next minute he was relaxed and friendly again as he turned to Pete and me. 'Anyway, we sent him about his business. I don't think we'll be troubled by him again.'

Ginger laughed nervously again and I wondered just how tough they had been with the young poacher.

'You two still haven't told us why you're here in the middle of the night,' Chas persisted. 'Are you on an adventure training course, too?'

'No.' I hesitated unsure as to how far we could trust them.

Suddenly Trevor grinned. His clown's face took on its former jokey look. 'I bet it's something to do with the gees?' he wheedled. 'Go on, flower. You can tell us. Remember, we like ponies too.'

# 14

## A pony to hide

I decided to trust the horsy youths. 'We're looking for a friend of ours. Mark Cooper,' I explained. 'He's run away from home.'

'But why do you think he's here?' Chas asked.

'I told him the old barn might be a good place to hide,' I added before Pete nudged me to shut up.

'The old barn?' puzzled Chas. 'Oh, you mean the boathouse.'

'It's not a barn,' explained Ginger. 'It's where the fisherman who lived in the cottage kept his boat. At high tide the water comes right up the gully.'

'I thought the ground was wet,' Pete looked down at his soaked ankles before glancing at me with a rueful grimace. 'Trust you, Pippa, to jump to the wrong conclusion. If Mark had listened to you and had decided to hide here he'd probably have been drowned.'

Still leading Magic, he advanced towards the old building. 'All the same, I suppose he just might be there. Perhaps we ought to check.'

'No one's there, chum.' Trevor moved ahead to bar his way. 'The place is just a muddy mess. You don't want to get yourself and the ponies dirtied up. You'll be in enough trouble as it is if your Mum and Dad find out you've been roaming the moors at this time of night.'

'You could be right,' Pete agreed. He turned to me before putting a foot into Magic's stirrup. 'Come on, Pippa. We'd better get back. Dad's apt to wake early in the morning. We don't want to risk him hearing us.'

As we rode homewards, Pete and I didn't talk much. We were tired and so were the ponies. Russet seemed almost to amble in his sleep; so much so that he put his foot in a rabbit scrape and would have gone down had I not jerked myself fully awake to get his head up.

At last we reached the broad path that led from Dunkerton Beacon and forced ourselves to keep up a steady trot. The fresh air and exercise seemed finally to have cured my headache but I could scarcely keep my eyes open and, at first, I thought I was dreaming when we heard the whinny ahead and a black shape loomed to meet us out of the darkness.

Magic called back, starting to jig so excitedly that Pete had his hands full to keep her in check. Even the sleepy Russet was roused. The trekking pony's ears pricked, his neck went rigid and his steps shortened. He high-stepped inquisitively towards the other pony.

Then the moon came from behind a cloud to silver the star on the stranger's forehead. His glossy black hide glistened. The intelligent thoroughbred head, close-coupled body, well-let-down powerful hocks and pluming tail made the newcomer's identity unmistakable.

'It's Hero!' breathed Pete. 'But without saddle or bridle – and where's Mark?'

'Oh, Hero!' I kicked my feet free of their stirrups and slid to the ground. Taking a piece of bread from my pocket, I approached the black pony with out-stretched palm. 'Here, boy!'

Luckily Hero seemed ready to be caught. When I grasped his forelock he did not even try to get away. He was co-operative, too, when I slid the strap of my haversack over his neck and led him beside Russet.

'What do we do, now?' I asked my brother. 'We can't take Hero home with us. Daddy would have to report him found if we did.'

Pete slackened his hold on Magic's reins and my pony blew in a friendly way to Hero.

'I'm trying to think.' My brother rubbed his nose. 'Hero's unsaddled and not wearing a bridle. That means Mark wasn't riding him, so he hasn't taken a fall and won't be lying somewhere injured.'

'On the other hand, Mark isn't likely to have turned Hero free on purpose,' I said. 'He'd be too afraid of him being found and handed over to Mr Finch.'

'That's right,' Pete agreed. 'Somebody else must have freed Hero. If so, that person may be holding Mark captive.'

'But who?' I puzzled. 'Chas and Co.?'

Pete nodded. 'I thought at the time their story about being out after poachers was a bit thin. They must be up to something they didn't want anyone to know about.'

'Perhaps they were intending to use the boat-house for some villainy,' I hazarded. 'Then, thanks to me, Mark came on the scene and spoiled their plans.'

'Could be,' he agreed. 'But there's nothing you and I can do about it on our own, Pippa. We'll have to wait until we can contact Dave and the girls and perhaps call on the chaps from the Inner Cities Camp to organise a rescue operation.'

'Meanwhile what are we going to do with Hero?' At the sound of his name the black pony nuzzled my pocket in search of more titbits. 'All gone!' I pushed him away. 'I brought only a single round of bread to help me catch Russet.'

'There's the barn in the Garlands' furthest field,' mused Pete. 'No one ever goes there. That might make a good hiding place for Hero.'

\*　\*　\*　\*

There were some forgotten bales of straw in the barn so we were able to make Hero comfortable. I'd allowed him to drink from a pond on the way and now I gave him a small feed of pony cubes from the rucksack. Meanwhile Pete was plucking grass from outside the barn.

'There you are, Hero.' My brother piled the grass on the floor for the pony to pull at. 'We'll have to leave you to it, but we'll come back later with some hay.'

First light was creeping over the countryside before we reached home. The world had gradually changed from the sharply-etched black and silver of moonlight to a dim, pearly grey. As we neared the Garlands' farmhouse the first rosy streaks of dawn were spreading across the sky.

The twittering chorus of the birds had reached a full crescendo, though the clop of the ponies' hooves on the stones of the lane seemed to echo loudly above it.

'Better turn Magic into the field with Russet and the others,' suggested Pete. 'Dad's such a light sleeper he's bound to hear if we take her down to the cottage.'

My brother held the gate while I led the two ponies through. Pippin and Cloud raised sleepily-enquiring heads as we took off Russet's bridle and unsaddled Magic. Then they dozed off again as, with an encouraging slap on their rumps, we sent our mounts to join their companions.

Suddenly, the peace was shattered by a flurry of barking.

'Go get 'em, boy.' Mr Garland's voice rose in a terse order as the black and white sheepdog, Glen, came bounding towards us. 'What do you think you're doing? Drop that tack.'

Through the dim light of dawn Dave ran to challenge us. Behind him came his father, carrying a shotgun poised to defend.

Pete and I looked at each other. We realised that neither of the Garlands had recognised us in the half-light and we were both wondering whether to flee or to stay and explain. Then Glen decided for us by recognising us.

The sheepdog's hackles dropped. He stopped almost in mid-bark. His angry rush became an ingratiating crawl. Apologetically he fawned up to us, tail awag.

'It's all right, Glen.' Pete stooped to pat him.

'All right, is it?' Mr Garland demanded. 'And what do you think you're doing, making off with one of my ponies in the middle of the night?'

'Easy, Dad,' soothed Dave. 'We thought you were the night-riders,' he explained to us. 'Dad heard me get up to investigate. Sorry for having given the game away.'

'What game?' Mr Garland glanced from Pete to me. 'What are you two up to, anyway? And do your parents know you're out?'

Pete shook his head and I hung mine.

'Well, then,' Dave's father decided. 'I'd best walk you back to the cottage. Your Dad wouldn't want you riding round the countryside at night.'

I looked up. 'Don't tell Daddy, please, Mr Garland,' I begged. 'You see, there's a lot at stake.'

'Such as what?' Mr Garland's brown eyes regarded us keenly. 'Why don't you tell me about it? You never know, I might be able to help.'

# 15

## Not fit to ride

'One at a time,' begged Mr Garland as Pete and I had both begun to explain. 'I can't listen to the two of you.'

'Mark came to the cottage this afternoon,' I said. 'Pete wasn't there.' I told how I'd fed Mark, given him some pony cubes for Hero and suggested he hid in what we had then thought to be the barn behind the Hidden Cove.

'The old boathouse,' confirmed Dave. 'It was used by an old man who fished from the beach. He kept his nets and gear there as well as his boat.'

'It was used for more than that,' Dave's father added. 'That boathouse has seen one or two cargoes of contraband in its time.'

'Well, we thought Mark could hide up there with Hero.' I brought them back to the point. With Mark perhaps even now in the hands of Chas and Co., I felt this was no time to go into the former smuggling activities of the cove, however fascinating they might be.

'So you think the three fellows who mistook you for poachers could be holding Mark prisoner?' Dave's father's expression was incredulous. 'It doesn't sound very likely. Admittedly their story about being after poachers sounds thin. Probably they were doing a spot of law-breaking themselves; poaching sea-trout in the stream, perhaps. I can't really see what grounds you have to think they'd kidnap Mark.'

'Because of Hero,' I said. 'They're all knowledgeable about horses and Hero's a valuable pony.'

'Maybe,' acknowledged Dave's father. 'Yet you didn't see any sign of the pony.'

'The pony wouldn't be there,' I began and would have explained that Hero had escaped had not Pete gently kicked my ankle.

'It's Mark you're really worried about, though, isn't it?' said Dave.

'Definitely,' said Pete. 'It would be best, Mr Garland, if you got on to the warden at the Inner Cities Camp as early as possible and asked him to set him up another search.'

Mr Garland seemed to be considering the matter. Then he said: 'That can't do any harm, I suppose. It all helps to keep the lads occupied. Right, Pete, I'll do that. Meanwhile, you two, be off home. I'll have a word with your parents in the morning.'

\* \* \* \*

Luckily Daddy had a job next day repairing a milking plant over at Yeoverton. Mummy went with him to visit the local market. They had an early breakfast and left at eight, so there was no opportunity for Dave's father to report our previous night's escapade.

Forcing myself awake in order to see our parents

off, I stifled the urge to go back to bed and make up for lost sleep. Instead I scrambled eggs for Pete and myself, phoned Dave and the girls and got ready to join in the day's search.

Dave, Sharron and Tracey were saddling Cloud and the two trekking ponies when Pete and I arrived at the farmyard with Magic.

'Dad's already been on to the police,' said Dave. 'They've promised to redouble their efforts. Meanwhile the Inner Cities Camp boys have been detailed to make a thorough search of the Hidden Cove area.'

'Which leaves us free to take a look at the cottage rented by Chas and Co.,' said Pete.

'I suppose so,' I agreed doubtfully, remembering the shot fired over our heads the previous night.'

'Don't worry, Pippa.' Pete gave my arm a comforting pat. 'We shan't let Chas and Co. see us.'

'A watching brief's called for,' nodded Dave.

Sharron eyed my brother speculatively. 'How's Pete going to get there?' she asked. 'Without Hero, the twins have only one pony between them.'

'I'll go by road.' Pete collected his bike which he had propped against the farmyard wall. 'See you at the Three Crossings signpost.' Pausing with his feet on the pedals, he added: 'Be sure to wait for me. We'll work out a plan of campaign when we see the terrain.'

Magic circled protestingly when I put my foot in her stirrup to mount. Poor pony! She was probably feeling as tired as I was. My headache had returned after the night's adventures. At that moment all I really wanted was to lie down and try to get some sleep.

Perhaps feeling so edgy made me too strict with my pony. Hopping, I managed to get into the saddle but I was still feeling for my off-side stirrup as I shortened my reins. Magic danced sideways and, unable to control her with my legs, I jerked her bit impatiently and scolded her. Unused to such treatment, Magic fly-jumped and I flew over her head and landed on the mud-caked cobbles of the farmyard.

Dave ran to catch Magic. Hearing a cry of alarm, Pete dropped his bike and came back to see if I was hurt, and Dave's mother, who had seen what had happened through the kitchen window, ran out to fuss.

'Not another fall, Pippa! I thought you were supposed to be resting after yesterday.' She took my arm. 'Come into the house with me. You must lie on our sofa and I'll get you a drink of hot milk.'

'I'm all right, really,' I protested. 'Let me go with the others. They may need my help.'

'I'm taking responsibility for you while your mother's out,' Mrs Garland said firmly. 'It's no use arguing, Pippa. You're not fit to ride. You need to rest.'

I pulled a helpless face at Pete. 'You take Magic, then. But remember to use the proper aids. I don't want all her training undone.'

'That's choice, Pippa, after what's just happened,' he retorted. 'Do what Mrs Garland tells you and rest – and don't worry. The four of us can cope.'

I hoped so. I knew that Pete and Dave were unlikely to take any foolhardy risks so long as they had Sharron and Tracey with them. Anyway, they had agreed that the best course would be merely to watch the rented cottage without being seen. Even so, I felt uneasy.

It was a mild morning and, through the Garlands' sitting-room window. I could see the daffodils in the orchard nodding in a gentle breeze.

The sun shone into the house and, after I had drunk Mrs Garland's hot milk and rested for an hour, I persuaded her that I felt better. 'I think it would do me good to be in the fresh air,' I told her.

'Very well. But don't go trying to follow the others on your brother's bike,' Dave's mother cautioned. 'Remember that nasty bang on the head you had yesterday. You still need to take things quietly.'

'I won't do anything strenuous,' I promised.

'Well, see you don't.' Mrs Garland's kindly face was concerned. 'Dave and the girls have taken a picnic but I'll expect you back here, Pippa, for lunch with Mr Garland and me.'

As I wandered into the lane I had no very clear idea of what I was going to do. Then a green-painted bus came round the corner and I read its destination – Stagcombe. It was a country shopping bus which would go right into Stagcombe, stop near the market and then return. Its route would take it past Three Crossings and the cottage rented by Chas and Co. If I went on it I would have a good view of the cottage from the high seat of the bus. I could stay aboard while the vehicle turned round in Stagcombe and be back at the Garlands' farm in plenty of time for lunch. Mrs Garland would be none the wiser and I'd have been able to satisfy myself that Pete, Dave and the girls had not run into any trouble.

Feeling in the pocket of my quilted jacket for the fare, I held out my hand to stop the bus. Dave's mother would be cross if she found out, but it was a chance I had to take. If the others fell foul of the racing three, I might be in a position to summon help.

# 16

## An unexpected clue

The bus bumped its way over the winding, moorland road. From its windows I could see gorse in golden bloom beneath the April sky.

Nose to the ground a small, brown dog quested happily across the heather, startling a curlew which rose into the air with protesting cries.

In a deep coombe, stood a group of hinds. Soon they would have fawns. Then, as the bracken croziers unfurled to grow tall, all one would see would be the occasional flick of an ear as the russet-coated deer dozed in the hot sunshine.

Round another bend, grazing ponies lifted their heads at the approach of the bus before galloping away, half in fright, half from the sheer joy of living.

On any other day I would have been entranced but now I was too full of fears for Pete and Dave and the girls – for Mark, too, wondering whether he was indeed a prisoner of Chas and Co. Those three horsy youths became more sinister the more I thought of them.

The racing scene attracted shady characters, or so it seemed from what I'd read. I thought, too, that Chas was too smart a character to associate with slower-witted Ginger and Trevor. Ginger had seemed pleasant enough on the two occasions we had encountered him but even good-natured youths could be led astray and apprentice jockeys might have more temptations than most. As for Trevor – well, he could be jokey and amusing enough but I had seen his quirky-lipped clown's face change. It had looked wary, calculating, even sly when he had diverted Pete and me from the boathouse, telling us how wet and muddy we would get and reminding us how annoyed our parents would be if they discovered we had been roaming the moors at night.

By the time the bus passed the Three Crossings I had worked myself into a real flap. I watched tensely as we rounded another bend. A low, white-washed cottage came into view. There was no other building in sight. The cottage had obviously been done up for holiday letting. Shutters had been added for decoration and the corrugated sheeting that had replaced the original thatch had been painted bright blue. So had the gate. The garden had been recently weeded. Primroses lined the path to the front door which was flanked by tubs of wallflowers and daffodils.

This must be the cottage that Chas had rented. There was no other. Even so, there was no sign of him or his friends; no sign, either, of the cream Mercedes that had so startled Magic the other afternoon.

Peering through the window of the bus I could see nothing of Pete, Dave or the girls or of the ponies. Then, as I watched, the door of the garden shed seemed to move. It opened cautiously and, while I was still looking, my brother's face peered round. Pete saw the bus and paused. Then, as we lumbered away, he came stealthily out of the shed, darted across the garden and dropped out of sight behind a bush.

So the others were on the job!

Obviously, finding the cottage empty, they must have decided to make a thorough search for Mark. So far so good! For the moment, Dave, Pete and the girls were safe. Now I had to worry only as to whether Chas, Ginger and Trevor might return too soon.

In spite of my fears I could not help being fascinated as the bus drove into Stagcombe. Before turning into the bus station it passed close by the market square and I saw the merchandise set out. There were clothing stalls, stalls of kitchen utensils and displays of furniture on the cobbles. Brightly coloured rugs hung from temporarily rigged lines. Tables were stacked with sides of bacon, hams, butter, bowls of clotted cream, eggs and other farm produce.

The cheese display prompted an idea. Daddy's birthday fell on Sunday, and he was very fond of cheese. I had over two pounds of my carefully-hoarded pocket money with me. It might be enough to buy Daddy a miniature Cheddar – a nicely rounded, smooth-textured, tangy little cheese all to himself.

Leaving the bus at the terminus I hurried back to the market, bought the cheese and was just crossing the road to the bus station when a blast on a car horn made me leap for the opposite pavement.

Glaring back at the car, I saw, to my amazement, that it was the cream Mercedes. Chas was at the wheel. Ginger and Trevor were in the back. They seemed to be wrestling as if in argument, but there was no sign of Mark.

If they had left Mark locked in the cottage, Pete and Dave would have found him by now. On the other hand Chas and Co. might have imprisoned him elsewhere. I was just about to memorise the car number when a hand appeared at the back window of the Mercedes and a packet was pushed out.

So Chas and his friends were litter louts on top of everything else! I was so indignant that I forgot about the car number as I bent to pick up the cigarette packet from the pavement.

As I did so I realised that it was not the usual sort of cigarette packet. Unlike the carton of the familiar British brands, this was a thinnish paper packet, untidily ripped open. Turning it over I saw an unfamiliar name – *Col des Montagnes*. French! It meant Mountain Pass. I knew that much from school. The manufacturer's address, too, was French: Rue de la Paix, Lyons.

Feeling that it might be important, I stuffed the packet into my pocket and ran for the bus. A French cigarette packet might not seem much to go on but it was the only clue we had. Was it possible it might somehow lead us to Mark?

\* \* \* \*

'It's as clear as school soup, I don't think!' My brother's brow knitted over the cigarette packet on his return.

'But it is clear, Pete.' For once Sharron contradicted my brother. 'Dave's father told us the Hidden Cove was once used by smugglers. Well, now it's being used for smuggling again. Chas and Co. must be mixed up in it. They got those foreign cigarettes from a cargo of contraband. Don't you think so, Dave?'

'It's possible,' Dave nodded. 'But how?'

'Couldn't a fairly large boat – a big cabin cruiser – put into the cove?' I suggested. 'The smugglers could get alongside the jetty by using the deep channel where Magic nearly drowned.'

'Too risky,' frowned Pete. 'If the smugglers came into the jetty they wouldn't be able to make a quick getaway. More likely they'd anchor off-shore.'

'And Chas and Co. would go out to them in a smaller craft to pick up the contraband,' I nodded. 'I can see it now. Perhaps Chas is keeping a rubber dinghy with an outboard motor in the old boat-house.'

'That would be why Trevor didn't want us to go in there,' my brother agreed. 'It all adds up.'

'But what are we going to do about it?' Tracey asked. 'And how will it help us to rescue Mark?'

'I don't quite know.' Pete put the empty cigarette packet into the pocket of his body-warmer. 'But I think we've got to show this to Dad. After all, he is a part-time coastguard. He'll show it to the senior officer who'll decide what action to take.'

\*　　\*　　\*　　\*

Mummy and Daddy were late back from Yeoverton; Daddy must have had problems with the machinery repairs. Anyway, Pete and I were both thankful our parents hadn't returned by the time we got back after a hasty but filling farmhouse tea at the Garlands'.

'At least we'll have time to see to Hero.' Filling a couple of hay nets. I slung them pannier-like across Magic's saddle.

Pete crammed his rucksack with pony nuts. Then, pulling his diary from his pocket, he tore out a page.

'We'll leave a note for Mum and Dad in case they get back before us and start to panic. Now what can we say?' He chewed the end of his biro.

'Why not put that we've gone up to the top field to check the fences?' I suggested. 'We can inspect the boundaries while we're there; then we shan't be telling fibs.'

'Good idea.' Pete scribbled briefly. Then he brought out the French cigarette packet and looked at it thoughtfully. 'I'm just wondering whether I ought to leave this now for Dad to see.'

'Time enough when we get back.' I took the packet from Pete and straightened it carefully. I was about to zip it into the pocket of my quilted jacket when I noticed a scrap of paper inside. I saw that it had been written on.

Inquisitively I drew it out.

'Look!' Smoothing the scrap flat, I showed it to Pete. 'There's some writing and a few figures. I wonder what it means.'

As he studied the paper he gave a low whistle. 'It's Mark's writing! It must be some sort of message.'

'Could be.' I remembered the scene inside the

Mercedes when it had passed me that morning. It had looked as if Ginger and Trevor were wrestling in amicable argument. But it might not have been friendly after all. The two could have been struggling with Mark, for instance.

'Perhaps Ginger and Trevor saw me and were trying to push Mark down out of sight. Probably he'd already written the message and was waiting his chance to throw it out.'

'And when he saw you he stuffed the note into an empty cigarette packet that they'd left lying on the floor of the car!' said Pete. 'Then perhaps he managed to push it out of the window.'

Smoothing out the creases, Pete deciphered the note. ' "Tonight. Hidden Cove." ' he read aloud. Then his brow furrowed. 'There are some figures. "Two-thirty" – that'll be a.m. and there's something else. It looks like "off-shore". Then this last bit's clear. It says "full moon".'

'So tonight's the night Chas and Co. are planning to land another cargo of contraband,' I said excitedly. 'Let's go and see to Hero so that we can get back and tell Daddy all about it.'

# 17

Trotting through the dark

'You two go to bed and stay there,' Daddy ordered as he struggled into his coastguard mac after supper that night. 'I've spoken to the Super, told him about Mark's note and he'll have passed on the information to the police.'

'But he'll only be concerned with the smuggling,' Pete pointed out. 'Pippa and I are worried about Mark. Do the police realise the smugglers may be holding him prisoner?'

'I've made that quite clear,' Daddy assured us.

'You can leave everything to the authorities, dear.' Mummy paused in the sweater she was knitting to make the point to Pete. 'You and Pippa have lost quite enough sleep as it is, roaming the moors until all hours. After Pippa's fall, too. We don't want any more of it. That's final.'

So Pete and I were packed off to bed. But not to sleep. I lay awake for hours, wondering what was going on at the Hidden Cove. I was anxious lest the police and the coastguards should move in too soon and scare off the smugglers without making an arrest.

Worse still, I was worried about Mark. Where were Chas and Co. hiding him, and how could the police rescue him without alerting the smugglers? How could they ensure Mark wouldn't get hurt in the show-down?

Pete told me afterwards that he had felt the same. Time dragged by with agonising slowness. The chiming of the grandfather clock in the sitting-room could be heard in our bedrooms. First it struck ten; then eleven; then midnight.

We heard the drone of the television. Mummy must have been watching a late film. At five past twelve we heard her switch off the set but still she didn't come upstairs.

She must be waiting up for Daddy, perhaps, too, she was anxious for news. Like us, she wouldn't be able to rest until she knew Mark was safe.

'Pippa!' Pete's voice was hardly a whisper as he quietly opened my bedroom door. 'Are you awake?'

'Of course.' I spoke softly. 'I couldn't sleep.'

'Nor could I. We can't lie in bed and do nothing. Let's get dressed, take Magic and Cloud and see what's happening.'

I hesitated. 'Don't you think we might ruin things? I mean Chas and Co. might spot us, call the whole thing off, and not keep their rendezvous with the contraband boat.'

'It would take more than spotting us to make them do that. Dad says there'll be thousands of pounds at stake. Smugglers don't give up that kind of money easily. Come on, Pippa,' my brother urged. 'Get dressed quickly and then come to my room.'

'Won't Mummy hear us going downstairs?' I protested.

Pete shook his head. 'We won't use the stairs. My window leads on to the scullery roof, re-member, and the covered water butt is just underneath. It's a blessing Mummy's staying up to wait for news. If she was upstairs and awake we couldn't hope to get out without her hearing.'

The bottom of Pete's window was up and I was just about to join him on the sloping roof when we heard the unmistakable sound of pony hooves in the lane.

*Five-and-twenty ponies trotting through the dark!*

The line of a poem about smugglers that Daddy used to read to me flashed into my mind. Daddy was very fond of Kipling and he'd pointed out how the rhythm was like ponies' hoof-beats. Only tonight, instead of twenty-five ponies there were only three and, instead of their being led laden with brandy for the parson and baccy for the clerk, they were being ridden. I supposed the loading up with contraband would follow later.

Pete and I froze in the moonlight as we made out the shapes of Chas, Ginger and Trevor, bareback without saddles but with clumsy old-fashioned bridles, astride Cloud, Russet and Pippin.

'Come on!' I tugged at my brother's sleeve. 'We've got to stop them.'

'Stop them!' Pete shook his head. 'Not likely! That would ditch everything. The coastguards want to catch those three red-handed.'

'Then what do we do?'

'Get Mummy to phone the coastguard station, of course.'

Chas, Ginger and Trevor were now out of earshot on the trotting ponies. We waited until they were round the bend on the cliff path. Then I gave Pete a hand to haul him up the slope of the scullery roof. He was half-in, half-out of the open bedroom window when there came a beam of headlamps from the lane.

A police car with flashing lights bumped over the ruts to pull up at the cottage gate.

Hastily Pete scrambled back into the bedroom. Together we crouched, just peeping over the sill, our ears strained to hear what was going on below.

A constable got out of the driving seat, followed by a sergeant from the other side. The sergeant opened the rear door of the car and held out a hand to help another occupant.

'Mark?' I whispered.

I recognised the lean figure. In the moonlight Mark's shock of brown hair seemed even more unruly. The shoulder of his anorak was torn and the strip of cloth flapped forlornly.

As he stepped out of the police car Mark stumbled and clapped a hand to his leg. I could see now why the sergeant had to help him to the house.

'Mark's hurt!' Pete was concerned. 'I wonder what Chas and Co. have done to him.'

'Let's find out.' I was half-way to the stairs. 'Then we can tell the police about the smugglers taking Cloud and the trekking ponies.'

In the sitting-room Mummy was urging Mark into an armchair by the fire. The logs were blazing but the boy's face looked pinched and I noticed that his clothes were dirty and black. His hands were trembling as he rolled up the leg of his jeans to reveal a congealed gash.

'That needs bathing and a proper dressing.' Mummy turned to me. 'Put on the kettle, Pippa, while I get some antiseptic from the medicine cupboard.'

102

While the kettle was boiling I took a packet of instant soup from the store Mummy kept for coast-guard emergencies and emptied the contents into a mug.

When I took it in to Mark, he and my brother were listening intently as the sergeant called police headquarters on his radio.

'We've got the lad,' the sergeant was reporting. 'Safe and sound but for a minor injury to his leg. He says he's had an anti-tetanus booster so there's no urgency about hospital treatment. Mrs Woodley's coping with the injury but the lad's badly shocked. Mrs Woodley says he can stay at the cottage until morning. Better inform his mother that he's safe. Meanwhile the Woodley children have seen the suspects pass the cottage with the three ponies. It looks as if they're on their way to the Cove. Let the Super know and contact the coastguards. O.K.?'

As he snapped in the aerial and turned to leave, I handed the soup to Mark.

'Thanks, Pippa.' The boy took the mug from me gratefully and began to spoon up the contents. 'Chicken and vegetable, my favourite.' He managed a shaky smile. 'How did you guess?'

'It's Pete's favourite when he comes home from football practice so I thought you might like it too.'

I perched on the arm of the sofa while Mummy started to bathe Mark's leg.

'Now tell us exactly what happened.' I said 'How did you manage to throw out the note? Where have Chas and Co. been keeping you? And how did you get away?'

# 18

## Happiness for Mark

'Chas and the others locked me in the coalhouse at the cottage.' Mark looked ruefully at his blackened clothes. 'That's why I'm so filthy. I was in there for hours.'

'But how did you get out?' I prompted.

'The police rescued me. As for the rest,' he sighed wearily, 'it's a long story. What really worries me, though, is Hero.'

'Then worry no more,' said Pete. 'Hero's safe. He turned up here. Pippa and I've got him in one of Mr Garland's barns. No one else knows,' he added hastily as anxiety flared afresh in Mark's face.

'Thank goodness for that!' Mark held his hands in front of the blazing logs. He had stopped shivering and already the colour was coming back into his cheeks. 'The police sergeant told me they'd tried to contact my Dad in the Gulf but he'd left. That means he must have got my message and be on his way home. If we can manage to keep Hero hidden until he arrives back, Dad'll be able to stop my mother letting Douglas Finch sell him.'

'Tell us what happened to you, Mark, after you left here the other afternoon,' I urged.

'I went to the old barn at the Hidden Cove as

you said.' Mark's voice was tired. 'Only it wasn't a barn. It was a boathouse and I didn't see how I could keep Hero hidden there. I was about to leave and look for somewhere else when those three pounced on me. Hero got away – I suppose that's how you came to find him.'

'He came back here,' said Pete.

Mark nodded. 'Anyway Trevor and Chas frog-marched me to the cottage. Ginger didn't seem to want any part of it. By the way, he's not a bad sort of chap, really.'

'Probably the others led him astray.' I had a sudden mental image of the young apprentice jockey's freckled face.

'Trevor's the real villain,' confirmed Mark. 'Him and Chas. Chas is the brain behind the scheme – and the money – a real smoothy. Trevor's greedy and cunning. He seems to have some sort of a hold over Ginger.' He broke off as Mummy came into the room with a pair of Pete's pyjamas and a big, fluffy towel. 'A hot bath's what you need, my lad, then you can have a sleep. I've made up the spare bed in Pete's room.'

'Let Mark finish telling us what happened first, Mum,' begged my brother. 'It's almost three already. A few minutes more won't make much difference.'

'Quickly then,' said Mummy and I could see that she, too, wanted to hear Mark's story.

'They kept me prisoner,' related Mark. 'Someone was always with me. Otherwise I'd have made a break for it. But they never let me out of their sight. I wondered whether Pippa would have told you she'd suggested I went to the boathouse and if you'd come looking for me.'

'That very night,' Pete told him. 'Then Chas and Co. warned us off. Next morning, I rode with Dave, Sharron and Tracey to the cottage to rescue you. After Pippa and I met Chas and Co. at the Cove the other night we guessed they'd be hiding you there. Only when we got to the cottage you were all out.'

'That was when we went into Stagcombe and I spotted Pippa,' explained Mark. 'Chas wanted to contact a pal of theirs. From what I could make out it was to arrange for the contraband to be collected from the cottage after they'd brought it ashore.'

'How did you manage to throw the note out of the car?' I asked.

'Well, I was sitting between Ginger and Trevor on the back seat. Ginger was dozing off and Trevor was listening to the racing on the car radio. I'd already scrawled a message on a scrap of paper and stuffed it into one of the empty cigarette packets they were always leaving lying around. When we saw Pippa, they tried to hide me, but I leaned past Ginger and chucked the packet out of the window. Full marks to you, Pippa, for realising what it was all about.'

'I didn't at first,' I confessed. 'It was sheer chance that when I was showing Pete the packet, I happened to look inside and find the note.'

'That's enough for now,' Mummy said definitely. 'Mark must have his bath and you two must go to bed. I don't want a cheep out of anyone until ten o'clock tomorrow morning.'

\*　　\*　　\*　　\*

It was half-past eleven before any of us awoke. We must have been exhausted because, as we learned afterwards, two cars had already come and gone that morning. First, the coastguard superintendent had insisted on driving Daddy back to the cottage after the eventual show-down with the smugglers.

Daddy and his colleagues had waited to inter-cept Trevor and Ginger as they rowed the contra-band ashore. A coastguard launch, aided by a police vessel, had boarded the cabin cruiser that had brought the cargo from France. Chas had been waiting with Pippin, Russet and Cloud to haul the laden rowing-boat to the boathouse. Then they made a dash to the cottage where the police were waiting. The police had taken the keys out of the Mercedes and immobilised the car when they'd released Mark from the coal-house and so Chas was easily caught.

The second visitor to Cliff Cottage had been Mr Garland. Dave's father had driven from the farm on the tractor to tell Daddy about the abduction of Cloud and the trekking ponies. He asked whether Dave could borrow Magic to ride over to the Hidden Cove and bring them back.

'I said he'd better wait until you were up and had your breakfast,' Mummy told me as I sat at the kitchen table spooning down cornflakes. 'I know you don't like anyone except Pete to ride your pony.'

Pete turned to Mark. 'We can use Hero, too, if that's all right with you. Then Dave can ride behind me and Pippa and Magic can take the girls. They're not very heavy.'

'Fair enough.' Mummy was dishing up bacon

and eggs from the frying pan. 'But you must have a proper breakfast first.'

We had just reached the toast and marmalade stage, and Mummy had put on a fresh kettle of water ready to dress Mark's leg, when the sound of a car horn from the lane made us all turn to the window.

'Oh gosh! It's my mother!' Mark's face tensed as he stood up. Then his taut expression changed to delight as the second occupant of the car got out and strode purposefully up the path. 'Dad!' He hurled himself at his father. 'Dad! Oh, Dad!'

Mr Cooper's arms tightened round his son and, for a few moments, they hugged each other while Mrs Cooper stood apart from them. Mark's mother was wearing dark glasses as if to hide the fact that she had been weeping.

In spite of everything, I was suddenly sorry for Mrs Cooper. Mummy must have felt the same because she took her arm and drew her to the window seat.

'Let me get you a cup of tea, Mrs Cooper. There's plenty in the pot. The children have only just finished breakfast as you can see.'

Meanwhile Mark and his father had finished their emotional embrace. Mr Cooper finally ruffled Mark's hair as he held him from him. 'Let's look at you. Now what's all this about? You've upset your mother badly; ruined her holiday; had half the police in the country looking for you.' His gaze swept to include Mummy, Pete and me. 'And no doubt you've put these good people to endless trouble. Now why? That's what I want to know.'

Mark gave his mother a half-apologetic glance.

'Douglas Finch was going to sell Hero. That's why he was taking me with Mum and him to Greece to get me out of the way.'

Now that Mark had begun to explain the words came tumbling out.

His father listened closely. So did his mother.

'I should have been firm with Douglas.' Mrs Cooper's mouth worked as she struggled to be honest with herself. 'Your father gave you Hero. Douglas had no right to sell him. Mind you . . .' She turned to Mark's father, 'I'm sure Douglas had only Mark's good at heart. He wanted him to do well at school, you see. He thought Mark was too preoccupied with eventing, spending every spare minute with the horse instead of doing his homework.'

'But I did do my homework,' Mark protested. 'I got up early to swot before I saw to Hero. Anyway, exams aren't everything.'

'You can't get far without them, son,' Mr Cooper pointed out.

'I know that, Dad. I realise I've got to get some qualifications but not the kind Mr Finch wanted me to have. I'd never follow him into the law. Never! Imagine ending up like him.'

'Douglas earns a lot of money,' Mrs Cooper protested. 'He's made a big success in his profession.'

'Who wants to sit in an office all day, suing people and arranging divorces?' Mark shot his mother a meaningful glance. 'I don't want to be like him, thank you, Mum. I'd rather be a show-jumper; and, if I'm not good enough at that, then I'll be an engineer like Dad.'

'You have to study to be an engineer,' Mark's father said firmly. 'I'm in full agreement with you having a shot at making the grade in the horse world, Mark, but you need something else to fall back on.'

Mark nodded. 'I know that. I'm not an idiot. I intend to do my best at my schoolwork. I'll try to pass my exams in maths and sciences while I'm eventing. By the time I'm eighteen I should have discovered whether I'm going to be good enough to jump professionally. If not, then I can go on to be an engineer. How's that?'

'Fair enough,' said Mr Cooper. 'So long as you stick to the studying. I shall want to see good school reports, mind, and no excuses. Meanwhile, we'd better get you home.'

Mark stood up. For a moment he did not speak. He just stood looking from one of his parents to the other. Then he dug his hands into his packets and kicked at the hearth-rug. Finally he faced his mother.

'If you don't mind, Mum, I don't want to go home. I'd rather stay with Dad, wherever he's going. Douglas Finch'll be pretty mad at me. I'd rather wait till things have blown over before I face him.'

'Mr Finch won't be at home, Mark.' Mrs Cooper took off her dark glasses and hugged her son to her. 'Oh, Mark! What have I done to you?' Over the top of the boy's head she looked directly at her husband. 'Douglas Finch is going to play no part in our future, I promise. I've been a selfish fool but I hope I'm not such a bad mother that I've forgotten how to put my son first.'

'Dad?' Mark turned questioningly to his father and as I saw the look on Mr Cooper's face I realised that neither Pete nor I had any business to be there. This should have been a private conversation between the three Coopers.

'Come on.' I turned to Pete. 'I can see Dave and the girls in the lane. They need us to help collect the trekking ponies.'

As I went from the room I heard Mr Cooper's voice. It seemed deeper and gruffer than before. 'It's up to your mother,' the engineer was telling his son. 'We'll have to see how things work out. For the moment, though, I'll come with you to Linden Lodge – if your mother can put up with me.'

\* \* \* \*

'Do you think Mark's parents really will get together again? For good, I mean?' Sharron rode Pippin alongside Magic as we trotted the ponies along the moorland track.

'I don't know,' I had to admit. 'I hope so, for Mark's sake. He obviously loves them both and with his father working away for long stretches as he does, Mark must need his mother very much.'

'If you ask me, Mrs Cooper's been a clot.' Pete looked over his shoulder to join in the conversation. 'Fancy preferring a dried-up misery like Mr Finch to a really smashing chap like Mark's Dad. She must be crackers.'

'There may be more to it than there seems,' I said guardedly. 'Mark's father's been away an awful lot. I daresay Mrs Cooper was lonely.'

Sharron straightened Pippin's mane. 'Anyway,

perhaps from now on Mark's Dad'll try to arrange his work so that he doesn't have to be away so much.'

'Easier said than done.' Dave urged Cloud to catch up. 'These days most people have to take work where they can find it. I reckon the five of us are lucky, all having parents who've been able to keep their families together.'

'Let's hope it'll be like that now for Mark,' said Tracey.

'Whatever happens,' I pointed out, 'things are bound to be better for him from now on.'

'And at least he's got Hero.' Pete put the black into a canter. 'Come on, you four, let's race to the next ridge. That'll give the ponies something to take the tickle out of their feet.'

As Magic sped between the clumps of golden gorse the sun came from behind a cloud. The sea turned to blue and two seagulls wheeled white against it. A lark rose from the heather to twitter high in the sky from joy of living.

I sighed. Shortening my reins to prevent Magic forging too far ahead, I crossed my fingers.

'Good luck, Mark!' I murmured. 'Be happy – you deserve it.'